AMALGAMEMNON

SELECTED WORKS BY CHRISTINE BROOKE-ROSE

AMALGAMEMNON
CHRISTINE BROOKE-ROSE

 DALKEY ARCHIVE PRESS / CHAMPAIGN AND LONDON

First paperback edition, 1994
Second printing, 2010

Originally published in Great Britain by Carcanet Press, 1984
© 1984 by Christine Brooke-Rose

Library of Congress Cataloging-in-Publication Data
Brooke-Rose, Christine, 1923-
Amalgamemnon / Christine Brooke-Rose. — 1st Dalkey Archive ed.
1. Humanities—Study and teaching—Fiction. 2. Women college
teachers—Fiction. 3. Prophecies—Fiction. I. Title.
[PR6003.R412A8   1994]   823'.914—dc20   93-21194
ISBN 1-56478-050-3

Partially funded by the University of Illinois at Urbana-Champaign, as well as by grants
from the National Endowment for the Arts, a federal agency, and the Illinois Arts Council,
a state agency

www.dalkeyarchive.com

Cover: design and composition by Danielle Dutton, illustration by Nicholas Motte
Printed on permanent/durable acid-free paper and bound in the United States of America

I shall soon be quite redundant at last despite of all, as redundant as you after queue and as totally predictable, information-content zero. The programme-cuts will one by one proceed apace, which will entail laying off paying off with luck all the teachers of dead languages like literature philosophy history, for who will want to know about ancient passions divine royal middle class or working in words and phrases and structures that will continue to spark out inside the techne that will soon be silenced by the high technology? Who will still want to read at night some utterly other discourse that will shimmer out of a minicircus of light upon a page of say Agamemnon returning to his murderous wife the glory-gobbler with his new slave Cassandra princess of fallen Troy who will exclaim alas, o earth, Apollo apocalyptic and so forth, or else Herodotus, the Phoenicians kidnapping Io and the Greeks plagiarizing the king of Tyre's daughter Europe, but then, shall we ever make Europe? Sport. Rugger. The Cardiff team will leave this afternoon for Montpellier where they will play Béziers in the first round of the European championship, listen to their captain, Joe Tenterten: we're gonna win.

I could anticipate and queue before the National Education Computer for a different teaching job, reprogramming myself like a floppy disk, or at the Labour Exchange for a different job altogether, recycling myself like a plastic bottle, and either

5

way I'd be a worker in a queue of millions with skills too obsolete for the lean fitness of the enterprise. Or I could hope for the best, which for me would normally arise out of dead men and women on a printed page, meanwhile anticipate on my severance pay if any and with my small savings make a humble down payment on a tumbledown small farm to go back to the soil as we all must, no sooner dead than briefly sung, to rear something or other, recycling weeds and words no sooner said than dung.

That would mean seeing the elegant portly man at the National Education Computer again who would during the burocrastinations try insistently to exchange a word in someone's ear for a brief place in my life which he will imply will fall into disuse without his aid. The new generation will supertouchtype programmes and games all to be superdevised by an elite of supertechnicians of communication I'll show you after hours he'll say.

Probably that would make the new generation the new high priests and oracles of pythian mysteries none will control himself or understand further, increasing gale eight, perhaps gale nine later, then becoming cyclonic in Fortes, occasional snow, good, becoming poor.

One day but not yet I might regret the clouding over of Orion whose doublesided sword so blunt so sharp will mar the memory of a menippean love. Soon the term will be over and Ethel Thuban will start up her chemicycle, gleeful at the clouding over and pouncing on my newfound plenitude. She will arrive on her motorbike and park it in the garage yard behind the block and press the bell marked Enketei downstairs and helplessly I shall let her come up.

Well Miss Inkytie she will say you should be apprised of certain facts which, I must warn you, may come as a shock to you so you'd better be relaxed and comfortably seated. Thank you how kind I'll murmur but she'll look around with distaste and criticize any changes she might notice or non-changes despite her insistent recommendations or perhaps praise something insistently as well. What a mess though, she'll boom, will you really be correcting papers in these dismal surroundings, why if you stay on here you'll be bound to go on undermarking mine, which you'll live to regret, for I'll take the entire bunch from the beginning to the principal and higher if necessary and so on and so forth. These attacks will unfortunately recur, only the tense pauses between them varying a little in length.

One pseudo-escaperoute might be the suave and portly man at the National Education Computer, who will wineandine me at expensive restaurants for the joys of deciphering the unfamiliar and tasting it with a palatalizing pause and a knowledgeable nod, which will be just like the teaching of literature I'll venture but he won't like that at all. Man will always eat, and drink, and take his pleasure he'll say, but soon he won't need to read about it as well, or even instead of. Will language ever give you the bouquet of this wine the flavour of this sauce the excitement of my desire at the mere touch of my knee against yours? It might I'd say, through the madlanes of memory and without the indigestion, but I'll feel a foolish flutter at fraternizing with the very force that will make my training my experience my lifelong passions more and more redundant, you mustn't worry he'll say and titillate my thigh.

If he were someone in a nineteenth-century novel I might ironically detach him.

Soon the economic system will crumble, and political economists will fly in from all over the world and poke into its smoky entrails and utter soothing prognostications and we'll all go on as if.

As if for instance I were someone else, Cassandra perhaps, walking dishevelled the battlements of Troy, uttering prophecies from time to time unheaded and unheeded, before being allotted as slave to victorious Agamemnon. But I had better use my severance pay if any which will depend on the National Education Computer to start a modest pigfarm, sacred to Aphrodite, where I shall trudge out to the sties at dawn light-headed for lack of sleep and the weight of a mammal moving through mud in cold clammy gumboots

7

empty of legs.

But that won't be in the main what she will wish to say to me, oh no, she wouldn't be one of those frustrated older women lashing out at everyone as I would seem to suppose with my knack of for ever getting but one third of the picture, she'll wish to speak to me about my psychological effect on her, would I be a witch, no, I wouldn't be that interesting it would be too easy. Yes Ethel but. It may interest you to know that I shall take all your comments on my papers to a psychographologist, whose name will have to go unmentioned of course, and who will no doubt discover once and for all where the fault would lie, nor can you do a flipping thing about it for let me tell you I shall keep them all, if necessary in a bank vault and if necessary prove it.

Here too in Athene's precinct will be the tomb of one whose name I would prefer not to mention in such a connexion. The marathon talks in Brussels will probably continue late into the night to determine what face-saving formula of cautious condemnation Europe should unanimously bring out.

And Willy will continue more and more sexplicitly to exchange his ponderous advice for a brief place in my life, so soon to become a dead letter without his benevolent presence, which for the duration of his desire would so easily mean I'd have no life but his, whatever that might be, a life of his pure pleasure, for he'll be a carefully cultivated confirmed bachelor, like me, though in his eyes the status that would be a trump for him would certainly be dummy for me. As such he at least won't offer marriage but only the dangling impossibility of it with many a tale of many a woman, each one imagining herself the one exception to his honest laying out of cards, begging him for that signal honour, even one in bed with him on the morning of her own wedding-day. And I shall ponder that he too should use literary means for dual satisfaction, each tale a boast and a warning.

If only Ethel Thuban could be as promising as this year's students, Anne de Rommède for instance or Chuck Cherryblue or Nelson Nwankwo or Hans, or else accept her

8

perfectly acceptable limitations. Nelson will surely become a diplomat and Chuck a poet of sorts and Anne, well, she'll plunge into the Leviathan of the Politics, the Physics, the Metaphysics, the Dialogues, the Republic not to mention the mediation of Master and Slave and all the rest, and emerge perhaps chained to a rock of ideology or else be carried off like Europe on the sacred cow of dialectics.

So don't try and turn the tables on me again by supposing me a frustrated woman lashing out Ethel will say or something like, for let me tell you I'll always have all I shall ever want out of life unlike you, nor shall I let you poison my mind, would you like some tea Ethel? What? Oh no thanks I shan't be staying, you, a childless and discarded woman who'll no doubt for ever compensate by criticizing everyone including your own students you should be encouraging so that either they will lose confidence or take refuge in an emotional crush which will satisfy your ego or have a nervous breakdown. So don't put on airs with me young woman not so much younger than me I'll bet for I'll have the backing of the principal and you'll be making a big mistake you'll be bound to regret some day in the future need I spell it out? This will be positively the last time I shall speak to you on the subject, it should give you fair warning. Goodbye.

Most of the allied representatives will disapprove of this speech, but the only one to raise his voice in protest will be Sosicles of Corinth. Upon my word gentlemen he will exclaim you'll be turning the universe upside down, men will be living in the sea and fish on land if you Spartans abolish democratic government and restore despotism in Athens. If you think it such a good thing for others why not give a lead by adopting it elsewhere? In the name of the gods of Greece, do not saddle our cities with despotic institutions. And if you refuse to desist from your purpose, if you still attempt to restore Hippias to power in Athens, contrary to all law and justice, you will have no support from Corinth.

After the Corinthian representative's appeal Hippias, who'll be more familiar with the prophecies than anyone, will swear

9

by the same gods that the day would come when Corinth would bitterly regret her stand, for she would find herself plagued by the Athenians and long for the Pisistratidae and long in vain.

The telephonist will ask what about and cut off my reply then come back and say hold on and I'll hold on but what to, then I'll have to repeat what about anyway when I'll get through to the wrong man, creating a false opposition as to the rightness of the right one and a false impression of relief when I finally get to him. And he'll invite me out again, the repayment for his trouble and expenditure will be sexplicit, he'll talk of my emotional desert presumably that he might do me the great favour of invading and irrigating it at will, apparently assuming a wilish game of playing hard to get rather than simple anxiety and a sceptical curiosity, or at most a redundant vague desire wholly unfocused therefore unfeminine until his fashioning passion should turn me into a captive on a small pigfarm I shall owe partly to him, super idea, your bankloan your severance pay my help with same, your courage your handywomanship and craftswomanship my car our brains our pleasure our fun. And I'll come down often, you'll cook me one meal and I'll take you out for the other, we'll explore the region, then we'll make love, all night, all night.

Birds of paradise a nature programme will murmur into my ear much later will flutter and flap to fly on the same spot in their courtship ritual, while gulls to impress their females will fly in formation and some in the south seas will do so backwards.

Could there be a sort of dynamic dedevelopment in types of amorous discourse?

After the news you will once again find your faithful companion of the night Nat Knightly with his splendid music programme. Goodnight and pip-pip-pip or will it be boom-boom or the World Service an hour behind the Cabinet meeting today, they will probably discuss, though it would seem unlikely that, and the emergency measures perhaps to be taken, and no doubt the agenda will also include something or

10

other to make the future possible, but there again how shall we hold it back, or forth?

Soon I shall be as redundant as to between desire and the infinitive and as embarrassing to the new society, unlike the seemingly wasteful ones and zeros in the sixteen or thirty-two or sixty-four bits behind the lightning languages of digital neotutors, with each his load of essential information in relation to the others, giving instant access to endless databanks and beautifully random memories. And in a little while the voice will announce the end of the World News.

We must err on the side of caution will say my knight-errant about the bank, not data, about the loan, not love, about the prospecting of tumbledown farms, not the prospective tumbling, for he will with portly elegance manoeuvre his way beyond the shudder of a doubt into my life and couldn't err on any side of any stepping-stone.

And yet the story which the people of Dodona will tell about the black dove from Egypt becoming their oracle would surely arise because the foreign woman's language would sound to them like the twittering of birds. And later the dove will speak with a human voice because of course the woman will stop twittering and learn to talk intelligibly. Similarly the young Scythians will be unable to learn the language of the Amazons but the women will succeed in picking up theirs, and therefore disappear.

Bolivia. A streetscape will flash on behind the electronic visitor to my livingroom and according to our correspondent in Santa Cruz who will suddenly stand facing us without a teleprompt but notes the terrorists in the British Embassy will probably demand the release of certain prisoners to be specifically named. The Foreign Secretary may at this very moment be putting pressure on the Bolivian government who will be asked not to yield to their demands. Iran. Another streetscape will appear and according to diplomatic sources the Smerdis on the throne may not be the brother of Cambyses at all but a Magus rebel. Sources close to the Cabinet will not comment, and neither will sources close to the Shadow

11

Cabinet. Next week however the Prime Minister will be receiving Cambyses King of Persia and no doubt the situation will be discussed, what do you think, John Carr, head and shoulders, well, certainly the presence of oil in the complicated psychology of anti-Westernism will make the volatility of the Islamic world especially perilous, with all the unforeseeable consequences we must expect.

Wouldn't it be better to make up a story in my head from time to time unheeded and unhinged? With characters talking: a diplomatic source will say, military sources will not confirm (the source will say), but industrial sources will suggest that Cambyses will therefore murder his brother for nothing, but the diplomatic secret will be kept under the Persian carpet, a government spokesman denying the rumour.

Meanwhile the Lydians, indignant at the murder of Candaules, will nevertheless agree that Gyges should continue to reign if the oracle at Delphi should confirm him as king, but that if the oracle should declare against him he should restore the throne to the Heraclids. The situation in Libya after the coodaytah will apparently remain shrouded in mystery until radio-communication can be re-established and we'll all go on as if.

As if, for instance, I were someone else, utterly fascinated beyond the slight flutter of anxiety by the gentleman bountiful who will bargain his vaunted power and portliness as un-attached male together with overrich expensive dinners as unquestionable advantages for a provisional invasion of my life, expressing his sense of sheer enchantment at finding me, despite my no longer young age and my intelligence, so wonderfully feminine.

If we were people in a nineteenth-century novel I could socially send him packing, like Emma Mr Elton, but in fact I wouldn't even exist, for today when pseudo-escaperoutes will so lightly turn sado-escape, and when women's very freedom will so easily be used against them by even moderately clever men I may incredibly have to go through the ludicrous motions of a mutual seduction simply to evade the tedious charges of society inside myself, which he will echo, old myths under new names, or the return of the repressed prodigal on pain of abnormal syndromes. But why should such charges bother me?

The answer will favour Gyges, while also declaring that the Heraclids would have their revenge in the fifth generation, a prophecy to which neither the Lydians nor their kings will pay any attention until its foolfilment.

And I shall be an infinitesimal decimal in the next statistics of teaching programmes cut, in graphs of national unemployment figures, European unemployment figures — but then, Europe, shall we ever make it? — world unemployment figures but the world, shall we ever make that?

Perhaps we should proclaim it an unemployment-deployment-free zone, then all the news could be given in the future, not just the agendas and state-visits and face-saving devices of uneconomic summits, and the electronic visitors speaking their videolects like substitute guests and husbands blandly conversing in our livingrooms might seem more real more flesh and blood than the fleshiest most rotund of flat characters. Or they'd be jerking yelling killing telling us to slim to eat cookies to save to spend to live it up to live it down to love to shoot to protest to obey and vote right left of centre. Why have television he'll say when you could have me and it'll be a good question meanwhile he'll find the women peace-militants so undelightful in their anoraks and thermal underwear and compare them to the elegant suffragettes. My smile will be a simile comparing them to explorers and soldiers in anoraks and thermal underwear as no doubt antarctic heroes, switch if off my love and come to bed. Perhaps I'll get rid of the television it'll save the fee. Perhaps it'll be the very redundancy of this or that ancient cultural guilt that will make me try so hard to want to be pygmalioned although for that it will be essential to go on seeming idiotic to prop the pigmylion and thus to disappear.

Wouldn't it be better to make up a story in my head unheeded, with characters talking, a government source will say, a scientific source will demur (the source will say), we shall soon be living exciting times. The characters should include a spokesman, a statesman, a chairman, a craftsman, a highwayman, a wo-man or wifman, but it will be safer to call them statespersons, spokespersons, craftspersons, highwaypersons, wifpersons, who will put spokes and states and wifs into their wheelchairs, careering around in their nomansland. Cabinet sources will make no comment and I shall mimagree, how should I not? Mimecstasy and mimagreement will always go together, like sexcommunication. Wouldn't it be better to mimage myself an Abyssinian maid, striking two small hammers on the cords of her dulcimer and singing of Mount Abora? Or a Cambodgean child? Or a New York streetsweeper or myself as foetus or as constellation, Perseus, Orion, Andromeda, Cygnus, Cetus, Draco?

Inland, east of Halicarnassus, the men of Pedasus will get warning of impending disaster through the priestess of Athene growing a long beard, I'll read to him to make him laugh and he will, and talk with his sidetrack mind impelled to impress of his own family descendance from Charlemagne, he'll have a genealogical chart to prove it. Will the twittering birds flutter out of the emperor's flowery beard? You mustn't worry he'll say and chuck me under the chin.

Meanwhile by way of exercise the Abyssinian maid will sing when I'll be born my primitive memory will be indelibly imprinted with the whale paradise that will expel me on to the shore of an unpromising land about to be torn apart. And won't all promised lands of milk and honey and all pleasure domes become battlefields of distant voices prophesying war by nation interposed, just like the other obscene?

There'll be my cranky curiosity, like Eve's the first scientific inkling to see whether the prophecies and threats would be fulfilled, whether the given model would fit the facts, precisely in nomansland where the male gods will ever take over the pythian oracles, turning them into twittering spokespersons. No doubt the agenda will also include some face-saving device for resolving political tension in the Middle

East like let us recognize one another before annihilating one another. Sandra my love of course I will he'll exclaim, and we'll celebrate when you'll be rid of the university, when thanks to me you will accept, and face, being only a woman.

A polar low will sneak down the coast depositing snow everywhere.

Soon the ecopolitical system will crumble, and sado-experts will fly in from all over the world and poke into its smoking entrails and utter smooching agnostications and we'll all go on as if.

Soon he will come. There will occur mimecstasy even if millions of human cells remain unconvinced and race around all night on their multiplex business, transmitting coded information, most of it lost for ever.

Soon he will snore, in a stentorian sleep, a foreign body in bed. There will occur the blanket bodily transfer to the livingroom for a night of utterly other discourses that will crackle out of disturbances in the ionosphere into a minicircus of light upon a page of say Herodotus and generate endless stepping-stones into the dark, the Phoenicians kidnapping Io and the Greeks in Colchis carrying off the king's daughter Medea, creating in advance as yet another distance which I'll have carefully to deconstruct tomorrow by letting him abolish all those other discourses into an acceptance of his, although

15

sooner or later the future will explode into the present despite the double standard at breaking points. We'll take that predge when we come to it.

And so what shall I be, Io for instance or Europe — shall we ever make it? — or a swinegirl sighing for her swineherd to sexplode the Lawrence myth, becoming cyclonic in Fortes, snow, good, becoming poor.

Meanwhile things will continue to be mildly pleasurable. Paris son of Priam will abduct Helen wife of Menelaus. Thus far there will have been nothing worse than wife-stealing on all sides, but as for what will happen next the Greeks according to the Persian account will be seriously to blame as militairily the aggressors. Plagiarizing young women could not, in Persian opinion, be a lawful act, but why make such a fuss about it afterwards? One should take no notice. For wouldn't it be obvious that no young woman would allow herself to be abducted without in fact wishing to be?

Soon the vulcanologists will fly in from all over the world and lean over the subterranean fire and take their soundings and make their calculations: I shall erupt within a week. The population will be evacuated. I may just continue to grumble like the population who will want to return to their crops and homes. Soon they will return to their crops and homes. I shall certainly erupt within anything from a year to a century. Perhaps I should walk dishevelled the battlements of Troy uttering prophecies from time to time unheeded. Perhaps I should allow myself to be abducted by a band of terrorists who will hold me prisoner in Oblitopia or why not right here?

Tomorrow at breakfast Willy will pleased as punch bring out as the fruit of deep reflection the non-creativity of women look at music painting sculpture in history and I shall put on my postface and mimagree, unless I put on my preface and go through the routine of certain social factors such as disparagement from birth the lack of expectation not to mention facilities a womb of one's own a womb with a view an enormous womb and he won't like the countertone at all, unless his eyes will be sexclaiming still what fun, it'll talk if you

16

wind it up, as if disputation were proof of my commitment, and he'll surely bring back my anchoretish emotional desert to remind me of his occupation and irrigation of it as signal honour but who will be deceiving whom on that particular playground?

Stockholm. According to a spokesman the government will not yield to the demands of the terrorists. Soon the psychic warfare system will crumble. Psychideologists from all over the world will lean over it and take their soundings and utter smoothing proagnostications and we'll all go on as if.

As if, for instance, I were some other constellation, not Enketei-In Cetus, not Jonah inside the Whale but Orion say, to be siberianized for flagrant delight of opinion.

Tonight the guard will kick me in the kidney or in the shin or trip me up snarling sonovabitchski or some slav equivalent or pestiferous peasant poetaster or cranial ukrainian or damned intellectual infrastructure, we'll soon see which, take off your shoes, open your mouth, show me your ass, let's see how many gold chippings, as if stealing gold from the mines of Kolyma could be of the slightest use to me after fourteen years. I shall be too emptied of strength and feeling to react to the guard.

The kitchen orderly will give me only one ladle of soup saying thin man thin ration, or no tasting for poetasters, or no eggs for eggheads, or rationing for revisionists, we'll soon see which, and my smile will be a secret simile. The rhetoric of repetition will protect me, for the mind must play to the last with anaphoric expectoration, waiting for which permuted variant day after day, week after week, despite the poverty of possibilities but no, it could be the kick in the shin and the egghead, or the tripping up and the cranial ukrainian, or the pestiferous peasant and the thin man thin ration or the kick in the shin and the rationed revisionist or show me your ass and your intellectual infrastructure, with so many elements the permutations of acute aching pain could be counted in thousands, but I shall not work them out for lack of a fidgetal computer and fundamental interest: Garbage In, Garbage

17

Out, my Gigo thoughts will always weave in and out of daily details such as the increasing wobbliness of my pickaxe or who will remember me outside if I ever get there.

My mind, for which I shall pay one more incredibly long year will save me and yet, engraved though it will be with every name of every prisoner, with every conversation about every fake trial and each invented crime and fabled treachery, will it retain all this, and if it does will it be believed, and if believed acted on or just sighed off as no concern of ours except as interference? And if acted on by whom and how, with all the vested interests in trade agreements, daytaunt or a merely cool war, the heat to be localized only in the de-developing elsewheres and somehow contained? Could there be any other solution but this brinkmanship to Lenin's prophecy that the capitalists' greed will always provide enough rope to hang themselves with, or else, all systems go, crumbling from inside and man starting again if at all ex almost nihilo? What then the biting frost and misery here against all that? Perhaps things will have changed by the time I get out. If I get out.

Tomorrow could well start with an early homonologue like sleeping alone again why, to be answered with a shrug and a smile like a secret simile, followed by his hohomonologue about the unfairness of nature, successful sex sending the man to sleep and waking the woman. As if sleepwaking alone were an accusation against sexcess rather than against my own excess to be for ever channeled into the mysterious voices of the night, gathering up solitude as a needed strength that will nevertheless be resented by one and all especially one, and so become a weakness, a heavy whale panting leglessly on a distant shore to give birth to a small profoetus in a flapping of fins before the final gasp. The ecozoologists will then fly in from all over the world and poke its entrails and fraudcast a stooging diregnosis and we'll all go on as if.

As if such solitudinous strength were not a newly to be developed organ of survival these solitudinous times when boys and girls will face the futureless featureless world and men and women of all ages and abilities may suddenly be deprived not only of a living wage but of a life's long loving gage. Read your feature in your stars.

Due to the monetenergy crisis, some specialist or other will reply to some question or other in the news, man will try to do more and more with less and less but there will be a painful transition during which he will do less and less less and less well if you follow me. And if I don't? Verbalizing if I follow him more and more towards a new satiety, merely displacing problems from recession to inflation and back again or from the daytaunt to the daybuckle of the thirdworld war? Peace then might come, as pure inhuman silence radioactive in the hushed fragments of exploded planet, which maybe some big dish telescopic ear will capture twenty-five billion light years away.

Meanwhile hello to one and all from your own favourite Nat the Nightman, I'll be with you till four a.m., in about ten minutes we'll play the detective game shall we, I'll tell you a story about our friend Inspector Briggs and his dumb assistant Sam Brown, we'll see if you can do better than ole Sam all you nightpersons, you'll ring me to give me your wild ass guesses, wags for short, hah, as to how the inspector will solve it and where the flaw in the ointment, hah, may lie, then as usual after three you'll make up riddles about your own home town and I'll have to wag and if I don't I'll fall back on two listeners, listening-aids, hah, to help me, who'll win a T-shirt and of course if they don't guess you'll win it okay? But let's hear a few records first shall we?

When will the unexpected cease to be foreseeable or vice versa? When will a political label spout an opposite catechism or a psychosociosexogenerational behaviour be unbehaviouristic? Or could the expectation generate the expected, which then and luckily will surprise us all with the pleasure of recognition?

Will Minny Sota have her litter tomorrow or Monday and will it be nine or ten or eleven piglets or more? Will the polls give the winning party a majority of twenty-nine seats or

19

more? Remember to switch on the spotlight above them to keep them warm in the pleasure of recognition of ma's tits before annihilation.

Soon they will sleep and snore, the other prisoners. Perhaps the prisoncamp should be a political asylum. There will occur the blanket bodily transfer to the central stove for an hour or so of utterly other discourses that will spark out of a flickering red glow upon the yellowing pages of a damp crumpled find on top of a water cistern, a miracle a paperback Herodotus, generating endless stepping-stones into the dark: should I declare you human or divine, Lycurgus? I would incline to believe, here in my rich temple, that you must be a god. Arcady? No, I will not grant it. Yet I shall not be mean and give you Tegea to dance in with stamping feet and her fair plain to measure with the line, dear Spartans. Creating in advance as yet another distance I shall have carefully to deconstruct tomorrow on pain of non–existence.

What shall I do when I get out of this brain-launderette where bouncing up and down I shall glimpse through the porthole the mad eyes of the headshrinkers who will forever watch the windows of the regimented machines for our glimpsing desperate eyes out of the bubbling babble? I shall be born again presumably as Orion on the seashore like Jonah out of the Whale. What will you be when you grow up? A maniac. Ego pyro sexo mytho clepto mono? No none of these but a graphomaniac — oh come that will include them all — to be imprisoned for graffitism as poor Cassandra will be enslaved by all Amalgamemnons and die with them not out of love but of amalgamation to silence her for ever.

But my words will carve through dungeon walls and I shall crawl priestlike through the hole into a neighbouring cell, carrying a secret about buried treasure, then montecristoid plummet as a faked corpse into the black sea of oblivion and swim ashore. At dawn I'll wake exhausted and write my cybernetic story of dissidence on the sand. The waves will wash it away. I'll write it again and the waves will wash it away again. That will be with the left side of my effaceable memory, for language in random access, but the right side will retain the space and the space music, carefully structured and pre-medicated, and I shall utter wordless poems with only rhythms and weird atonal leaps along the gamut of all the possibilities. Below that or over and above it will operate the second memory, indelibly imprinted with my escape despite deletions that will be irrecoverably lost, an engine hurtling into a black and endless void, where I shall steal a boy and put him on my shoulders to guide me east or westwards walking across the sea. Or else to be carried off by Eos the new dawn and slain at last by Artemis. What will you be when you are reborn? A schoolboy in the school of the future. No, not the usual school of afterthought rearranging history past and present in the light of national self-esteem for political ends and means, in this one only the future will be taught. The highest marks will be given, not to the most correct which will be unverifiable but to the most ingenious.

Let men do more and more with less and less or less and less less and less well, the faster the media the slower their reactions in the rush with which they will speed through history. Let a and b stand for mutually exclusive hypotheses, extrapolate and develop. Take it from there, write in future Adish on the geophysics of hunger the demography of fear the ethnology of injustice the cybernetics of desire the economics of violence the technogymnastics of diplomacy the psycho-engineering of information the vulcanology of revolution the mythopath-ology of politics the ecology of knowledge the gnostology of nostalgia, every existing field and others to be invented, can you imagine, if we take the kids young enough, what future men and women not to mention persons we shall make? But first I have to get out.

I must get himself out. Meanwhile the ecopoliticonomists will fly in from everywhere and poke the entrails of the grunterranean fire and mutter smoothing pragnostications and stake out their statistics to announce the coming recovery, the summit in unemployment figures will be reached in about nine months and we'll all go on as if.

Sleep will not come, and I shall read Herodotus out of passion perhaps listening to Nat the Nightman or Dial Dolores or Dan the Man of Dawn or vice versa, sharing it for the moment only with a prisoner on the other side of the globe made out of myth and memory and multitudes. Out of passion perhaps or to keep in tenuous touch with the father of fibstory that will soon vanish for ever as topic to be taught or thought in the dedeveloping country of Europe to be so clumsily kidnapped on the sacred cow of technoideology above and mass redundancy below.

The problem of automation, Willy my present Amalgamemnon will announce between the shrimp cocktail and the fricandeau, will be what to do with the totally brainless. Perhaps I might say to respond a whole series of jobs will have to be kept uneconomically manual for charity, which will breed more dependence and hate. But I might not reply since some brains such as mine will soon be declared as redundant as some brawn, unless to be recycled into a text-processor at some future date we must hold back, or forth, as long as possible. Or else he will with the ponderous conviction of a government official in the know approve the nuclear physicists' report on the five hundred percent safety measures and hundred percent human safety record compared with mines and oilrigs and I shall tenniswatch his teleprompting eyes and mimagree, unless I take the other side on the nevertheless far greater potential danger and so fill the space-time till his departure. So that even apart from humane error and waste disposal the nuclear will continue to be unclear until all too nuclear in the longshort term but will the long or the short term fuse or fiss?

Meanwhile he'll speak without thinking and I'll think without speaking or vice versa but never quite together since my speaking to any purpose other than sado–elegant pub-lounge platitudes will already begin to make him angry, or at least uneasy. Soon the plane of vision will take off through the fog into a dull grey screen of bright green frames and phrases, but meanwhile the millions of politicopsychobiological cells will remain unconvanquished and race around on their multiplex business transmitting secret information, some of it infinitesimal to the nth decimal and to be stored away perhaps among the things I shall never know such as the back of my mind or who will be the next man to sail round the world on a log.

Tomorrow he'll say Sandra my love when shall I see you again I'll be free tomorrow, I'll be free Friday Saturday Sunday. Friday Saturday Sunday I must prepare my classes correct papers no I must weed the vegetable garden clean the pigsties wash my hair meet Orion invent Andromeda from time to time unheeded and unhinged discover the grammar of the universe.

If woman be the warrior's rest should man be the warrior of her rest? Will his seduction always mean her reduction producing the inducement to reduce back, rather than fungame of equals in a futureless world and not as need, could sex as open-eyed choice of half a mind to opt for other riches from time to time unheaded unmanned unpersoned not yet be deemed also a woman's privilege now despite the viceversatile myth of man's deep independence?

In any case, why should three distinct women's names be given to a single landmass? According to many, the name of

Libya would come from a native woman and that of Asia from the wife of Prometheus. As for Europe, who will ever know if it be surrounded by sea or where it could get its name from unless from the Tyrian woman Europa, but Europe, shall we ever make it? Or will this or that sovereignty continue to stop imports of this or that for a wrongsized label or to pour lorryloads of eggs artichokes grapes taperecorders and videolects upon the roads?

Meanwhile things will continue to be mildly plausible. Overall the thaw will go on, although there'll still be some wet snow falling over high ground, but clearer weather will follow later to reach the Dover Strait around the end of the period. From Start Point to the Isles of Scilly and north to the river Eridanus, flowing into some northern sea, where amber may come from, the winds will be mainly light southerly, freshening and becoming south-east tomorrow over the Tin Islands.

Wouldn't it be better to read a story in my head from time to time unheeded, with characters talking, a spokesperson pursuing a chairperson for instance or vice versa who will love a highwayperson who will attack a statesperson and take her to wife until the wifperson become a statesperson again and the highwayperson console himself with the spokeschairperson or vice versa.

That would be most unconvincing but for whom? During the night the winter seeds will push a little upward with the late February aprilshowers, or filaments will form stars and all at once I'll see a crowd a host of golden aphrodisiacs. The colza in the field east of the cottage or east south-east will change from small cabbage-like plants to tall gangly ones ready for their May display of brilliant yellows. The maize in the northern field veering west norwest will already be a foot high, preparing the wall that will block me from the road all summer so that I shan't be able to see oncoming traffic if any. According to Mr Jolly and the rotation of crops he will plant his maize south of me next year, backing south-westerly before becoming cyclonic.

South of the marsh country the Egyptians will eat bread

made out of sacred grain, and goosemeat and beef, but never touch fish, nor will they ever sow beans, imagining them unclean, or even eat them when growing wild. Could I but find them growing wild Orion will think bitterly I'd be amazed and delighted to pick them for my soup or get a fish dish for once, however thin the ration and whatever the permutations of expectorations. The men of the marshes will gather lotus-flowers when the rivers flood the flatlands. They will pick out a kind of poppyhead at night in the dying light of the stove and bake it into a loaf of sanity and survival, and I shall also eat the root, round and big as an apple and sweet, and place the boy on my shoulders as a poppyhead to guide me eastorwestwards across the water to regain my sight.

At least you'll have to admit a war between England and Germany or Germany and France would now be inconceivable, my Amalgamemnon will say in earnest contestation of some general remark during the beef strogonof or some other vast meal I shall have spent hours preparing by way of implicit exchange for his wineandining that will no longer be sexplicit currency but assumed as mutual pleasure from apéritif to post pousse-café, or some such irrefutable datum he will present as highly controversial before the rest of the routine the washing up the undressing the chucking me under the breast with a cluck of his palate on his way to the john.

And as to Europe we would seem to know more about the eastern side of it through the Scythians. And round the Black Sea, if we except the Scythians, will be found the most uncivilized nations in the world. North of the Scythians would be many tribes, including the Sauromata whose wives, descendants of the Amazons and Scythians, will apparently ride out with their men. Then, after many tracts of emotional desert and nomad tribes will be found the Issidones, an extraordinary people in that men and women appear to have equal authority. It may be among the Issidones that the strange tales of the distant north might originate, tales of one-eyed men, and for Herodotus they'd have to be one-eyed if women have equal authority, and of griffins guarding the gold, and of

Hyperboreans. Let me add, however, that if Hyperboreans exist beyond the north wind there must also be Hypernotians beyond the south.

It would certainly be a hypernotion to go back to my spindryer or my brain will be too wet for me to trip a neat iambic step and drily utter the expected wooden truths without drenched irony as heavy as sarcasm. My poppyhead theory will work only in the short run of a few more months to go.

The pretence, however, will not outlast his desire.

In the long run of sixty million years the ice age will cover the earth if it survives our incipient iceaging indifference. But first in the short run it will wrap itself in its shortwinded bad breath so that the poles will melt, in fact a mere boob of a blubmarine could cause this anyway which would at least stop the emotional desert's intractable middle-earth spread. In sixty years there could be sixty metres of water in Red Squared or, before that, will the long term or the short term fuse or fiss? But then in sixty billion years or less the sun will become a red giant and gobble up the solar system and slowly shrink into a cold and black fullstop.

And before that, tomorrow for instance, Professor Albireo Cygnus will lecture at the Moscow Academy or shall we say M.I.T. on the future of the sign, he will lean over it, cygnans/signatum for he will have his little joke, and posteriorly read into its entrails like a soothsayer.

Will any of it still be there next time he'll look at it? And if not, well? well, then I shall walk in with my hypotheses and sweep the detritus of civilization.

Swing low sweet chariot, collecting the garbage. But not so low as all that, for I shall have walked off with all the prizes, top of the prisoncampus, holding them in a pile that will rise high above my head like a Pisan Jacob's ladder I shall climb spine by spine then kick away platonically when I shall have reached the ultimate foreknowledge, which being ultimate will be knowledge of nothing that could follow.

And what will you be then, Orion?

A secret agent patient, denying rumours. I shall have to reinvent them before I can deny them for all the rumours will have vanished from the face of the earth as will all ritual and therefore all meaning. A woman will make soft eyes it will not mean love me, a man will make software promises it will not mean hard wear, a finger will beckon it will not mean come to me, a stream will flow it will not mean drink me, a booted man will arrest you it will not mean he'll have evidence of your guilt, a teacher will press a keyboard it will not mean he'll have knowledge to impart, a newscaster will appear in your living-room it will not mean believe me, a priest will raise his arms it will not mean God'll be alive and well in Atlanta City. Oh there will be signs but multitudinous readings as a perfect compromise between respected mysteries and scientific incertitudes.

Thus the Spartans, alas for ambiguity, will lose the battle for Tegea and wear the very chains they will have brought for the enslaving of the Tegeans, and with the line they will measure out the fair plain of Tegea as labourers, as I shall measure out the galleries of the Kolyma goldmines or the corridors of stately homes for, how long, two months, two weeks if the random access memory of Moscow find me at all. By the time of Croesus however the priestess will promise them Tegea if they can find the bones of Orestes, in Arcady under Tegea where two winds will blow, easterly force seven and westerly force five, there will be smiting and counter-smiting, and woe on woe. That earth will hold the son of Agamemnon. Bring him home and you shall prevail over Tegea.

During the noche oscura heavenly bodies will become heavy bodies on a measurable radius to yield pendulum laws that will replace constrained fall or some such radiotalk, not that this will resolve anything and heavy bodies will become foreign bodies and kings will become cabbages or pigs with wings unless cabbages become kings and woman become the wifperson in man and man the husbandry in woman, the future become past and the past present —

Whose voice could that be?

— and the blacks return to Africa and dance a host of golden afrodizzyacts —

Beirut. The tension will continue to mount as the negotiators will go shiating on. During the night the bulletins will repeat themselves, slightly altering the emphasis, doing more and more with less and less then less and less with nothing. People will ring please save our embassy our flag our honour which maybe will turn out not to be ours at all and everyone will lose interest. The bulletin will quote a government spokesperson who will deny the rumour circulating but no one will acknowledge the circulation.

Perhaps like Orion I should image myself as a government spokesperson denying rumours, all those rumours from the other obscene which predefer to be stifled from sweet pollution in the slow gas-chambers of civilization until the return of the repressed prodigal. Perhaps I shall become a child again like his poppyhead boy and tame the nightmare of the huge small hours if I sleep again as an engine hurtling into a black and endless void. Then I would dieborne. More likely I shall merely dream of the diminishing cat I would have forgotten to feed or love, who will be living backwards shrinking to a furry foetus like my oh my prophetic soul my uncle ego, pouring his poison of oblivion into the ear of sleep.

Beirut. The hostages at the German Embassy will be released if the Israeli government free six Palestinian prisoners whose names will not be publicly divulged. Listeners will no doubt sigh with relief at this rectification of conflicting agency reports. But Europe, shall we ever make it, feel it? Listen: I promise. Will that always be the same returning discourse of the prodigal parent, lover, politician, prescripting a more analgetic administration of worldly goods with goodly words and galluping vote inventions? Be vocal not equivocal. Vote for us now and at the hour of our death, making the Abyssinian maid for instance sing when I shall reach puberty my parents will marry me and get three camels in payment. I hope they will choose Mussa and not Mustapha. I hope Mussa

28

will have the camels. Mustapha may become the strongest and the richest and the biggest but Mussa will invent his strength and riches in talisman tales tatooed with half-told taboos and tambourined on tendrons with tangible tenderness and tensile tones.

Meanwhile things will continue to be mildly pressurable. Take the yolks of two eggs, place them in a seed bed between Start Point and Eridanus, gently press them in, add salt and pepper and a cupful of fresh modifiers finely chopped, blow in a westerly girl force four, lightly drizzle twice a week and transplant in June. Speak softly to their poppyheads and they will love in bloom as a poppycockcrow.

That might well be my crowing achievement, slowly articulating all aspects of the current subparadigm as Orion might say, achieving the anticipated in a new way. But of course the forecast might not be accurate, the temperature might rise forty-eight hours later, election and courtship promises will be quietly forgotten or transfigured into rising prices and controlled information to purge the economy so as one day to trigger it off again. The ever-returning prodigal discourse will always be Listen: I promise. There will be minor variations to frustrate viewer-expectation within the episodic, prices for instance will be controlled and unemployment raised or violence controlled and popular spirits raised or discontent prebirth-controlled and violence multiplied by a coefficient of information aborted in one school of after-thought and hyper-tropheyed in another. The theororists will kidnap very important perceptions and hold them up to ransom then killem in cold blood for lack of direlogue. When I grow up I'll do you down. We'll take that grudge when we come to it. Nor would I be surprised if with the army of Xerxes consisting of 5,283,320 men, the rivers should some-times fail to provide enough water. As to food it may well give out, for if the daily ration for one man be kept to no more than a quart of meal, the total daily consumption would amount to 110,340 bushels, without of course counting women, eunuchs, pack-animals and dogs.

A man perhaps or a wifperson will sail round the world on a monologue.

Soon the errorists will plagiarize a planeload of idées reçues and hold them up to ransom but crack troops will fly in from all over and crack the code and vengeance will ensue. Andromeda might be on the side of the errorists. Yes, I could well imagine that.

One day perhaps but not tonight or for some time I shall create Orion, and perhaps Andromeda weeping for the oblivion of Orion whose petty sword will always mar the memory of a manypaeon love. Never let anyone see you foresee them, keep quiet Cassandra, forecaster of your own pollux, keep your castrations in perpetual cassation for nothing will ever be exactly as you shall one day see it in retrospect, otherwise you would grow big with expectation and sexplode, the expected generating the expectoration or vice versa perhaps. Qui vivra verra, che sera sera, you shall see what you shall see and may the beast man wane.

Mr Jolly the farmer will look up at the sky and say the arvest 'll be late this yur an it don't look like warmin up for many a week yet, and I'll be workin me ole bones to conkers for nowt you mark my words, for all we're likely to get for a bushel o corn or a gallon o milk this end o the disturbution line. And another cow spectin an she won't push neether, like tother before er, oncount of all that them straw fer fodder in the drought I'll warrant, nor the calf won't push neether an this bull e will makem too big. My missus and me'll avter drag im out again wi ropes and een then e'll lack fer air an flop down, e won't stand up at all at all, een to suck, an we'll avter bottlefeed im again till e does I'll bet. What wi one waterless yur an one flooded an sunless altogether what'll the world be comin to it'll be all them things in space if yer ask me.

You mustn't worry Mr Jolly I shall say Willy-nilly, things won't be that bad, you won't lose two calves one after the other it wouldn't be fair, which won't be true or logical and he'd know it as well as I'd know Willy's patronizing lies so I'll quickly fill the air with Willy-intentioned intendancy and ask him if he'd like to come and see Minny Sota and tell me if I should do it better. Eleven of them just think. And it'll be the turn of Minny Apolis soon. Look at those cuties. Will they be warm enough under the one spotlamp? Should I hang it lower? I'll clean Sinsy Natty's sty tomorrow. Oh yes I'll manage, with these well-drained sties and the big broom and hose, but if you should have a moment to come over and help it would be lovely.

Nevertheless quite soon the vet will come, to operate the cow moaning immobile at the other end of the field and bring out the calf which won't get itself born even with Jolly and his wife tugging at the rope tied round its peering hooves. Will he come in time? He'll have to work in the floodlights of his car at the other end of the field, elbowdeep in blood and placenta. The cow like Europe may die but he may save the calf if he can inject it in time to compensate the loss of oxygen during the unmuscular struggle to get out. When I finish the pigsties I'll have to run out there and see, glad that Minny Apolis and Minny Sota and Sinsy Natty won't give me that kind of trouble, only a preponderant disposition to crush their progeny to death.

Soon I shall get out. If nothing goes wrong, like a new accusation or wilforgetfulness. What shall I do? Will anyone recognize me? How shall I trace my relatives? Shall I be allowed to do so or shall I be exiled as undesirable or be kept in some caucasus of muted dissidence, schizoided in a dizzydance for ever? But variation could clear the pipeline. Maybe the best way to make the future possible would be a letter such as Dear aunt Liz,

If you still remember me you will be pleased I hope to hear that I shall be flying to England from Hamburg this summer, after several months of trying to locate you since my release. May I come and visit you? How are you? Well I sincerely trust, despite the years. It will be great to see you again and I shall have much to tell you. Please write to the above address.

Your loving nephew,

Orion.

So they will constellate from nebulae, elliptical, spiraloid. I could cheat of course and turn to the last pages of the world as book and therefore find myself still inside the Whale, In Cetus, Mira Enketei, why not, but Mira will do, a small star varying from third to ninth magnitude in a comparatively long period of eleven months, during half of which she will be invisible to the naked eye. Mira will thus be considered by astronomers as the only mildly interesting feature in an otherwise tedious constellation which will rise due east and cross the southern sky in autumn, in advance of Orion, sailing on Eridanus. Whom I shall call Orion Rigel, in love with Anne de Rommeda.

He should be Perseus of course, rescuing her from her rock by killing Cetus the sea-monster, but let us not complicate matters, for though I'd like to keep Orion to myself by now, I'd rather give him over to her instead of Perseus my murderer and survive.

Quite unlike me she will be real, in other words a modern intellectual, for tragedies and histories and pigs and prophecies and cabbages and kings would hardly count as real, or modern, or intellectual, but quite like me she will be passionately so. What circumstances besides her activity on committees for his release, her beauty and their propinquity would pit those two together in Milano I could well imagine as electrical, the explosion if not of matter and antimatter then of dialectical materialism and delectable metarealism, meeting neither left nor right but plumb at the extreme centre. And who will speak there without thinking and think there without speaking but me?

Their vectors will intersect four times like two crossed doubleyous or two crossed Cassiopeias, forming a mesh of wires, backing north and south in an eastwest dialogue. Her vector will proudly descend via Lombard and Frankish princes from Charlemagne or so she will surprisingly remind him at the third intersection, relating, she will say, to all the reigning families of Europe and thus, as he will inevitably see her, to be carried off and up, for who could be stupider than Jupiter, on the sacred cow of ideology towards an oversynthesis, and apt therefore to sink again into amalgamud. His vector will rise from peasant poet singing of cows and ploughs on stately farms towards a hard poetic justice in cybernetics, then carry down again on a tractotalitair of truth as traitor to reality then up through the hard labour of sick stately homes some archipel ago. The first point of intersection will be the word lost in admiration, the second passionate love with no ground to stand on, lost to eternity, the third the clash, lost in repetition, the fourth the breaking point, lost in silence. Anna my love, Anadyomene he will exclaim, my Annalects of delectation.

Rionek! Why always play with my name, she'll ask, gently perturbed by the shift in identity.

All words should be played with and names most of all, he'll answer but she'll say for fun yes, not all the time though, or you'd undermine the fragile fabric of communication. Why he'll come back quick as a flash, would you separate fun from communication? Well, because, well, no I wouldn't, and she'll laugh with him and cuddle up to him then add because there might be no ground to stand on if you didn't at all. And glancing up at his quizzical downward gaze she'll murmur, perhaps according to you there won't be?

Because, he will enounce slowly and softly, you will believe in the absolute truth of your words and I shall for ever be lost in the absolute relativity of mine.

Don't be absurd, she'll snap, I shall always, from my very profession as political commentator and writer, be aware of the danger of words, but why would you increase their frailness with constant play, even with my very identity?

Your identity he'll ask, or your profession?

You'll never quite take either of them seriously as equal will you?

But yes, as seriously as you will, until you yourself won't.

Wouldn't that be just another way of patronizing me she'll choke, as if you said, 'you'll see, you'll grow up out of your owlish solemnity and learn my subtle sense of shifting meanings'.

Oh Anna, Anna, your sensitivity will always touch me and trip me up, like the soft catch of breath before the first foot in a paeon of praise, a poem as complex as a sonnet and as immense as an epic, oh my Anna Crusis.

Oh they will make it up, often and every time. He will apologize, profusely, kiss her tears her lips, she will smile and say forget it but never will. Her letters to him in Hamburg will be fuller than ever of the books he must read, programming with ideology his newfound freedom from its consequences.

As for Onomacritus, collector and editor of oracles, he will carefully omit any prophecy of setback for the Persians and choose for Xerxes only the promising ones, about how the Hellespont would be bridged by a Persian and how the army would march from Asia into Greece. His example should perhaps be followed, in fact most leaders even today will kill if not the messenger of bad news at any rate the message.

Meanwhile things will continue much the same which will be reassuring to many. The politicopsychobiographologists will lean over the volcano and take their resoundings and calculate the grumblings by gallup pole and thousands will die or suffer elsewhere of invasions wars defeats murders executions forced tributes famine slavery, the Argives and the Athenians, the Babylonians the Geloni the Dorians the Egyptians and the Ethiopians, the Zacynthians, the Thebans the Thracians and the Thessalonians, the Ionians and the Indians, the Kretans and the Kyprians, the Lydians the Lacedemonians the Medes the Mylians the Mysians the Ninevehans the Orthokorybantes the Pamphylians and the Paphlagonians and the people of Palestine in Phoenician Syria, the Rhodesians the Samians the Scythians the Xanthians, the poor Psylli who will declare war on the south wind and be buried in sand, even perhaps the Opidians on Cyrus's route to Babylon. Then a letter will be sent saying My dearest long lost nephew,

I shall be overjoyed to see you again. You will surely be much changed after such a long and terrible ordeal. But then you will find me much changed also, indeed positively aged. Will you have news of your parents to give me? Please come any time, but ring me a little ahead at the above number or write. Will you be coming by road rail or air? I shall have to give you instructions if so. Greatly looking forward to seeing you.

Your ever loving aunt Lizvieta.

Will you be a maniac or a soothsayer or a patient agent denying rumours? If so I shall have to instruct you in the realities of repression and terrorism, repression always coming first although this will not mean that I shall have knowledge to impart except turn left into your language lobe turn right into your space and music lobe leap up a tall scale then down into a black and endless void indelibly imprinted with fore-knowledge of paradise lost and promised after the next election if you vote right left of centre or seventyfiveyear plan if you do not vote at all. Will Ferrari prevail at le Mans? Will Billy Battleboy win the middleweight championship at New Orleans? What could be wrong with British football economics rugger cycling employment policy tennis trade unions parliament shipbuilding poetry skiing agriculture high technology novels cars investments food pop music incomes policy will be the agonised questions for many a year.

The marathon talks in Brussels will no doubt continue late into the night to try and work out evergreen structures for green Europe and find out whether it can ever really be green or only black and blue.

And Willy will wittily produce as revelation and proof of my apparent unwillingness to accept his views when supposedly contrary to mine instead of merely obvious, the way that kings and leaders will kill the messenger of un-welcome news. *Vale!*

And if you want a girl you should eat more calcium, if a boy more protein, or make love when the womb is high hello can you hear me?

Yes yes, go on my dear.

After the full moon, and he'll get in deeper and make a boy, could that be bzzzz.

Oh, could we call back our listener? Maybe you'd like to answer her question meanwhile doctor?

Yes indeed, but what strangely patriarchal notions, they would seem hardly better than in Hippocrates where the male child must of course come from the right side of both the man and the woman, so that women must make love in a certain position and men must tie up their left testicle, as a woman I must gently protest. I'll tell you one thing, though, it will always be the father's chromosomes that will determine the sex, and science won't change that, nor will husbands ever again be able to put away their wives for not producing a boy. But soon it'll be possible to sort out the father's spermatozoa and neutralize the XY chromosomes, then inject, as it were, a decoction of daughters if you should so wish, although the ovule may still not accept it.

Or a broth of boys?

That may also become possible, but the male Y chromo-some may prove easier to neutralize than the female XX.

Why should that be? Hello? Ah, would that be our lost

36

listener again or another? Yes, ask your question please.

Well, er, don't you think that if everyone could choose wouldn't they all want boys and upset the demographic balance? For the name of course.

Dear me, how long will this deepset phallocratic thing continue, even in our women?

Well I would agree with you doctor, but my husband, he'd surely want a boy, or several, and as for me, well, people will also choose girls surely, for the pretty dresses and dolls and pink cradles and the balance would remain the same especially since wars won't just kill men.

So you'd see the choice as a matter of consumer goods and the reason as destruction rather than desire?

Well, if women had their say, but men'll want the name to go on.

The name. Yes, but why shouldn't women keep and even transmit their own name?

Excuse me doctor but do you mean matriarchy?

No Mr Burgeon, each child would choose.

But wouldn't that mean civic havoc?

But the transistor will probably get knocked off the sty partition by the hosepipe and fall into the pigdung. Soon there'll be no need even to meet, for lack of dialogue, all the smells swells lips hips eyes thighs kisses caresses will be transmitted through electronic devices to partners on request and the war will be over at last at least that one, no possessiveness no jealousy no demolition no power games no loathing from the quick death of desire no love no tenderness. Achieving the anticipated in a new way. As in our push-button sex. At sundown I shall go in and selectronically devise a wild excitement by prestidigital touchtyping and invent myself an alternate family, mythical magical multitudinous and play with names and thus anteprogenitize:

John Jones

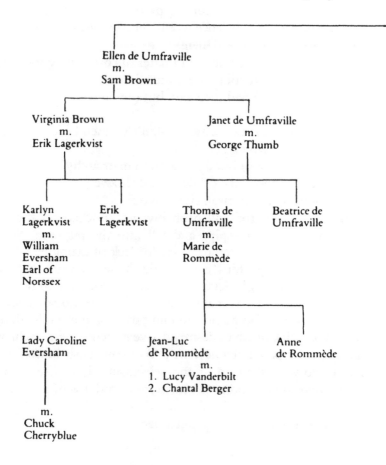

Ellen de Umfraville
m.
Sam Brown

Virginia Brown
m.
Erik Lagerkvist

Janet de Umfraville
m.
George Thumb

Karlyn
Lagerkvist
m.
William
Eversham
Earl of
Norssex

Erik
Lagerkvist

Thomas de
Umfraville
m.
Marie de
Rommède

Beatrice de
Umfraville

Lady Caroline
Eversham

Jean-Luc
de Rommède
m.
1. Lucy Vanderbilt
2. Chantal Berger

Anne
de Rommède

m.
Chuck
Cherryblue

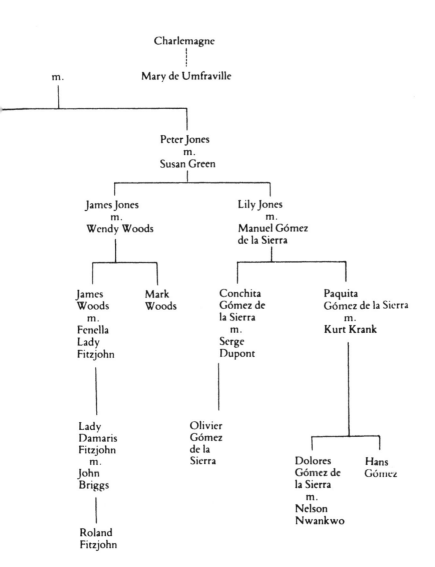

Or any other permutations to be put through the fidgetal imputer. In this particular reversion it would seem that the Joneses and such would gradually disappear and we'd no longer have to keep up with them. Oh crap, these days all the kids would choose to remain Green Brown and even Red.

And why should Lily prefer Jones to Green and Tom prefer de Umfraville to Thumb? Why will Erik Lagerkvist and Mark Woods not marry? Will one die age nine or be a priest or a homosexual? Will Beatrice de Umfraville be plain ugly as the only explanation for bacherlordom, as opposed to free choice for a man? Where will Karlyn meet the Earl of Norssex? Will Nelson Nwankwo be Nigerian or Ghanean? Will Kurt Krank meet Paquita on a neo-fascist secret mission to South America?

What passions rages disappointments what loves hates failures sufferings successes sacrifices what senses and sensibilities prides and prejudices from time to time could be revealed. What a fanfair of strumpets what auburns golds jet blacks what liquid eyes fair bosoms soft silks velvet waistcoats stiff collars hard mouths jangling bracelets snarling tones smart uniforms battle bereavements gay twenties financial crashes miners' miseries heroics in the sky black invasions deprivations liberations jazz revivals new cars new looks hippy looks punk looks blue jeans black leather black gòld black moonstones blue notes red brigades whited sepulchres promised lands denied rumours short bad breaths melting polarities revolutions revelations revaluations revolitions revillusions redundancies could be provoked evoked revoked, what whales hydras dragons serpent-bearers lyres lynxes lions scales ploughs and charioteers could be constellated.

Unlike the Lycians, who will have no choice but will always take the mother's name not the father's. Ask a Lycian his name and he will tell you his own name and his mother's, then his grandmother's and so on. And should a free woman have a child by a slave, the child will be considered legitimate whereas the children of a free man, however distinguished he may be, and a foreign wife or mistress will have no citizen rights at all. Or as somebody like Solomon might say and will, Beware of foreign wives they will bring ideologies.

Soon the harvesting will start, Mr Jolly will be busy with the collecting of the colza and the sowing of the last maize crop, and the days will be longer and I shall have more time. One day but not just yet Anne de Rommeda might regret the clouding over of Orion whose doublesided sword at the third intersection will always mar the memory of a manic pagan love, although she'll plead for tolerance and peace and so will he, saying he'd never ask her to share his hard-laboured convictions but only to respect them and not to toss them aside under easy assimilations.

What assimilations she will ask astounded.

Assimilations he'll answer containing his anger, whereby everything he might say will remind her of, be reminiscent of, smack of some unmentionable yet all too frequently evoked political labels soon to become totally meaningless from the very assimilations, and if he might say so part of the deep unconscious indoctrination of Western intellectuals, a new trahison des clercs, and she will look at him in amazement fury and deep distress, not know what on earth he might be talking about she'll never assimilate him, simply his surmise that she'd be on the side of the terrorists will be strongly reminiscent, no, she'll mean be exactly like the usual gambit over here whereby everybody will begin every dialogue with the declaration that they couldn't, of course, be in favour of the cold-blooded execution of adversaries or of blowing up innocent holiday-makers sky-high, but the gambit will usually be employed by the very people who'll mobilize public opinion in favour of restoring the death penalty —

Amalgamemnon, he'll murmur, more sadly in control by now.

What on earth — can't you forget literary allusions for a minute?

Go on.

No she'll say she'll never be on the side of the terrorists but she'll see the genealogy of events as a constantly widening spiral of repression — terrorism — repression — terrorism and

41

she'll know for a fact that this will always start with repression. So let me enlighten your political innocence —

Please don't. Look Anna, let's not go on like this. Give me your hand. Calm down. And listen, just for a minute, if you will allow me to express myself.

But of course.

That some should call me mad, or bought, or corrupted by the big capitalistico-imperialist powers under the guise of cybernetic firms in Europe would be admirable if those same people could confront the unspeakable mentalities whose far-reaching implications won't ever be wholly understood until too late, or as long as it may remain more comfortable to pay lip-service only to such belief. The worst would seem to be that some could in fact be confronting them unawares in the praiseworthy name of the wellbeing of the greatest number, or worse, knowingly unwitting, a kind of blind spot —

But I don't disagree! Where will all this lead she'll interrupt me. To showing up my ideology as a blind spot as opposed to yours?

That would be childish I'll say, we'll all, always, have blind spots. But we could at least try to open our eyes to them, to become aware at every instant of the possibility. By all means exercise your leftwing intellect my love, and write good books, important books, but be open, not slogan-minded. Stop equating metapolitical with innocent and even ignorant. If you must plonk me to the right, think of me at least as a rightwing hard-labourer, though I shall always think of myself as a truer revolutionary than many, and will remain so, and live out my contradictions, metapolitical or infra or whatever. But please try to avoid your amalgamations, which couldn't possibly be your own or else I couldn't love you.

Well, she will snap then, you couldn't.

The boot may be on the other foot I'll say gently or you wouldn't go on hammering at me with your dialectically materialized syntheses of contradictions on the mere grounds of a newly acquired enthusiasm for a rather old method.

Old shouldn't necessarily mean discredited she'll gasp.

No, unless you slide asyntactically, oh my Anna Coluthon, contesting the principle of contradiction by misusing the term to cover conflicts, confusing contradictions, which will not cover all the possibilities, with contradictories, which will, inclusive with exclusive disjunctions. Soon you'll be unable to see the good for the theses.

I'd be tickled, I'll ironize out for her, that you should try to use a dialectical argument with me, if it were any good, but unfortunately it won't wash, for if you examine it you'll find it lacking —

I should hope so I'll murmur

— even in the traditional Hegelian moral imperatives that should be minimally present, as well as profoundly political in its apolitical dodge, like everything you'll be likely to say. As one of your friends here, whose name must go unmentioned, and so forth, in a sad dialogue of the deaf.

On this lake the Egyptians will act by night, in what they'll call their Mysteries, the Passion of that being whose name I will not speak.

Mummification would seem to be a distinct profession. The embalmers will produce specimen models in graded and painted wood, the best and most expensive will represent a being whose name I must forbear to mention in this connexion. The best process will be described as take a dozen abstractions, mix with fresh modifiers finely ground, take an injunction, transgress it with a sharp knife and simmer it slowly in a westerly ghoul force four with three blind spots and a soupçon of fact. Let it cool and add to the mixture, season, fold in the froth of ten well beaten tracts and cook for twenty years at romantic agony then allow to cool, serve with frosted doubt. Doubt of course will always be a luxury in a society run on certitudes, and next week I shall give you a recipe for the simmering of exquisite doubts.

Orion however will be more knowledgeable than I and talk of three-dimensional tabular models that will carry, from node to node, in all directions and along multiple connexions with many possible entries, a given flux of any reaction what-

43

soever, each quantifiable. And he'll compare it, rightly or wrongly, with the poverty of the dialectical model which will carry, along its linearity, only one univocal type of determination consisting of the classic negation, opposition and surpassing, the undeniable strength of which nevertheless cannot be evaluated or quantified but only grossly maximalized, thus reducing all conflict to the old game of Master and Slave, but what the hell, doublethinking without speaking or doublespeaking without thinking, whose side should I be on?

Tomorrow at breakfast why breakfast Willy still half asleep will grapple with some bristly topic such as the foolhardy courage but ignorance of citybred intellectuals in the backtothesoil movement especially of course women who will never be really suited to farmwork unaided and alone, not that he will propose to join me in it thank goodness with his portly elegance, unless it be his other and more wistful argument that man's own technology will finally deprive him as warrior huntsman fisherman builder ploughman of his last superiority, why, with spermbanks he will be reduced to a mere studbull servicing a herd of cows, why bull and cows I'll say to avoid what he'd call a real discussion why not hog and sows, well, if you like, and we'll laugh and I shall feel oddly affectionate and play the objectingaim as woman objectoy why it'll talk if you wind it up what fun his eyes will say sexclaiming, as if any disputation were proof of my commitment.

But maybe I'll mimagree if only for the wifman's rest, too tired to explode the Lawrence myth just now. Could love as constancy of ambivalence and not as need still be a masculine privilege, could mimicreassurance of a man for the ritual of it and sex as open-eyed choice of half a mind to opt for other riches from time to time unheeded be in fact a woman's secret strength, as yet to be denied on pain of frigidity or other ascetic and therefore aesthetic preferences to be turned into accusations? Could man be stubborner about the undesirable in him, vainer, less proud? Or could it be a sort of blind courage that women will always lack?

That I shall always lack, knowing in advance that my very strength will always and every time be my ultimate weakness because desired disguised. Others would be more skilful, less intimid-dated into undisguise. But no, the distribution of self-deception must be asexual.

And who would you be talking to Sandra love?

To people my world of course, the millions of neural cells politicopsychobiological that race within the spaceship of my mind inarticulating some other woman that will distart quite soon between Start Point and the Scillies with a westerly girl force seven. I shall always laugh at the absurdity of the map-makers who will go on showing Ocean running like a river round a perfectly circular earth, with Asia and Europe the same size. According to Darius's campaigns into India, Asia must be surrounded by sea and bear a general geographical resemblance to Libya, which must certainly be surrounded on all sides by sea except where joining Asia.

As to Europe, shall we ever make it, green red or black and blue, shall we ever know whether or not there could be a sea to the east or to the north-east of it? Nor will he ever guess how instead of whining and dining vague desire out of kind cowardice or cowed rememoration of once upon a spacetime I could at the drop of a batting eyelid be so much more real, skeletally digesting my rodent hunger in a black child's swollen belly, screaming my yellow terror under the unloading underbellies of loud monsters tearing up the sky, storing up red resentment in my deadskin reservation, gripping a desiccated hand to plunge naked and wrapped in psalm into refinal solutions or icily tallying out my time for breathing untotalitairily. But Thursday he'll turn up unexpectedly Sandra my love let's make love and maybe I'll reply I must correct these last exams or rather I must feed the pigs clean Minny Sota's sty, weed around the leeks mend the roof treat the rear wall for damp.

Oh lordy, really you might organize your work like me to be free for my visits. Yes and you might realize that you could come less often uninvited and less long. Oh, you and your damn pigfarming experiment. And pray how would I live without it would you prefer me to be still teaching humanities elsewhere or to have spent my savings and severance pay on something quite other not going through you, why, you wouldn't even know of my existence, think of that, as I might, often.

He'll look confused for he won't mean that at all and he'll watch me look around, would you have lost something?

Yes, that terrific initial admiration for my pigfarming experiment and general capacity to cope alone, could you be hiding it under your sweater and he'll laugh, come, let's not quarrel, what would you like to do then shall we go for a drive and then have a gorgeous dinner in that restaurant by the river?

So that you can make a grandiloquent magnodrama on the dirth of the right mustard and the decline of good service among these peasants of the Danube you old dinersore? Whereon I shall feel guilty and affectionate about deep fulfilment with man as the salvation of woman, although my very happiness without him, to be so besieged, will very soon be black-marked against me as pretentiousness, as would even now a merely quiet hint that life with him even discontinuous would seem more limited and less fun than life with students friends or colleagues or even life with pigs and magic stepping-

46

stones. So that more or less happily but much too late at night I'll go clean out the pigsties imagining myself a streetsweeper in lower eastside New York.

Tomorrow I shall journey forth to find work and freedom and evasive eyes in the big city, collect the garbage of the wastemakers or sweep destreetus of civilization. Where e'er you walk my broom shall dog your feet. Tomorrow there will be a thirtythirdworld congress a famine colloquy a northsouth dialogue a non-aligned summit a palacetime piecemeal conference.

For although like you I could be a spokesman denying rumours from below that predefer to be stifled till the return of the repressed prodigal, I could also be a streetsweeper cleaning up the unmanuring dung dropped from above, which will have to be collected up and sorted out and recycled maybe into serviceable goods, as in psychoanalysis, a genie from a plastic bottle. When the magic cycle of genuine shit will have been replaced by the chemicycle of pure electronic thought ever expanding, more and more unbiodegradable, the heart of the earth will stop, shrivel to a curled up foetus to be ejected lifeless and wither to a moon without even the attracting planet to encircle except the distant sungod dead because unseen unfelt by anyone.

Mussa however may be killed in this terrible war unless he dies of hunger but then we may all die of hunger. Soon I shall feel too weak to work in the fields and pound the meal with the other children and old women. Even my younger brother will soon join the rebels in the mountains. And if we survive and if peace should ever return no doubt Mustapha will come back, not Mussa, and he will claim me without camels even. There will be no tales tatooed with tangy tangible tenderness and I shall be pregnant only with a heart-beating despair.

Some oubreaks of rain and drizzle will spread from the west with good visibility becoming moderate so perhaps I shall manage to drop him gently before that, perhaps I should try again soon, then clearer, mainly dry weather with good visibility will follow around midday, flowing into some northern sea, where our tin and amber may come from. Because if Willy with his grand and portly elegance and even grander portlier certitudes and already semi-obsolete burotechnics not to mention manners may soon appear to me in certain ways as a charming dinosaur doomed to extinction, I with my unemployable and quite obsolete humanities and interpretive doubt will undoubtedly appear to him as a diplodocus bringing forth the next ice age merely for not wishing to spend so many of my days and nights with him for the duration of his desire which apparently won't abate yet, why this intensity, why want it all at once all of the time surely a gourmet of his refinement should like a humanist appreciate the harmony of well ordered elements? But that would bring about the usual cataclysm attributable to humanistic error, which I shall fall over forward gymnastically to neutralize, seventy times seven dissembling if he disassemble me then quietly and secretly reassembling myself later. Diplomatic sources will refuse to comment. He will call my transistor and its multiple disputations on all topics great and small my lover substitute and he'll be dead right, for I shall spend the clearest of my nights with him and he will soothe and stimulate me without complaining or demolishing if I disagree or fall asleep. He'll be like fictions only somehow real.

Meanwhile things will become more than mildly pressurable. Vulcanologists will fly in from all over the world to calculate the time of my eruption. Which will remind me, Ethel Thuban should soon be starting up her chemicycle of accusations, turning me again into her whipping boy and wailing wall, dividing the city, a sitting target for her unclear missiles, unless somewhere along the line I send salvoes back, to be then pounced on as carping, criticizing and complaining, or else I'll beg for peace, to be pounced on as profoundly unhappy and clearly suffering from abnormal syndromes. Which will be true in a way if she be a syndrome. Yet how long turn the other cheek to sheer cheek, that will be breathing fire and brimstone? Or even not?

Well, Miss Inkytea she will say, so you too, like everyone

else, would seem to be about to fall again into the same mantrap, which, I warn you, may come as something of a shock, or which, perhaps, she'll beg me to reconsider and snap out of it. Do you really suppose you'll find happiness with a weekend sponger? She will arrive on her motorbike and look around the kitchen of the tumbledown farm with distaste. What a mess. Modern pigsties in the hangar and a slum inside how typical.

Would you like some tea?

No thanks I can't stay, oh well, if you're going to pour the water anyway, and she will call upon me to stop trying to have it both ways, rearing my baby-substitutes yet clinging to my false image of her as a clot of dubious intelligence who'll never make it in the world without guidance from me, though that would be but a third of the true picture and I of all people should know that every story will have at least two sides. So how about packing it in and having a bash at a spot of human kindness eh? You may not believe this she'll go on before I can reply but if you go off with this man and we should part I shall best remember you grinning like a Cheshire cat at every damn remark I might make about anything at all, indeed for all I know that grin will soon become your stock in trade, your automatic response to all and sundry and much good may it do you. Need I spell it out?

No, please don't.

You cannot play both your beau role as cultural mother-instructor and your role as tragedy queen for ever having her life invaded and her peace shattered or being buggered about in some way if you'll excuse my language unless you find yourself another sidekick.

More tea? But she'll wave me away or say well yes and go on. In this connexion I intend to practise what I'll preach, so to speak. You will never, never catch *me* urging, much less instructing you to snap out of it and learn your lesson and all that crap. I hope I'll resist the temptation ever to refer to the damn thing again. Stay with it till the rest of your days if you want, and much joy may it give you.

Well I —

Forgive me for saying, however, that I shall long regard it as a monstrous way to treat anyone at all. To quote someone at college whose name must go unmentioned I'd venture to hope for your own sake that the darn thing will peter out soon and that you'll really once and for all learn your lesson as you apparently expect me to learn mine. You can't put on airs with me, though let me tell you that you'll be making a big mistake if you don't snap out of it, which you'll be bound to regret some day. This will be positively the last time I shall speak to you on the subject. Goodbye.

When the Samians reach Sparta they will procure an audience with the magistrates and make an interminable speech to emphasize the urgency of their request. The Spartans however will answer that they can't remember the beginning or understand the end. So the Samians will try again. At the second sitting they will bring a bag and merely remark that the bag will need flour, to which the Spartan magistrates will reply that the word bag would seem superfluous. All the same, they will decide to grant the request for assistance and the Spartans will begin their preparations for the expedition.

Soon the big bumblebee buzzing outside will lurch in again and obstinately try to extract pollen from the painted flowers on the glass door leading to the washroom in the old dairy. It will hesitate, remembering then deleting again the fact that even I as mere human would be incapable of painting pollen just as I couldn't make the twittering of birds with words nor a taste or a smell but at best a madlane memory of it, weeds burning for instance, or the warmsweet hammy smell of pigs, or wearing perfume of jasmine rose essence and catgut or fumigating myself like the Babylonians sitting over incense after intercourse. Unless I get myself embalmed de luxe so that the brain will be extracted through the nostrils with an iron hook and the rest rinsed out with drugs, the flank will be cut open with a flint knife and the contents of the abdomen removed, the cavity will be washed out first with palmwine and then with an infusion of pounded spice, then filled with pure bruised myrrh, cassia and every aromatic substance except frankincense, and then it will be sewn up again, after which my body will be sunk in natrum for seventy days then washed from top to toe and wrapped in strips of linen smeared on the underside with gum.

In some distant field to the north, Mr Jolly's tractor will gently pollute the quiet of the countryside early in the afternoon. Soon there will be no more trees sticking untidily out of the hedges around the fields for he will cut the last few down to regain a yard or two of sunny and unrooted patches despite the regulations and Willy's intendancy-toned explanations about destroying microclimates. The sparrows and the starlings around the cottage will pick out all my heartsease and impatiens seeds from their boxes and surely turn purple and yellow and pink and red, fluttering in the wind like flowers, tied to a stalk and unable to fly.

Unless like the phoenix I bring my parent home in a lump of myrrh all the way from Arabia and bury the body in the temple of the Sun. This I would do by shaping some myrrh into a sort of egg as big as I could carry, then hollowing out the lump, putting my father inside and smearing the myrrh over the hole, so that the egg-shaped myrrh will then be the same weight as originally.

One evening when the summer comes my friend the toad will come out again to listen entranced to music out of my lover substitute. He will venture a little nearer for Beethoven Bach or Monteverdi, his prehistoric pachydermic surface slowly emerging from under the hydrangeas. His throat will throb, his bulging eyes will blink to modulations then close. He will stay for classic jazz folk and pop but crawl away from hard rock and hillbilly, with a hesitant waddle, one long hindleg lagging behind at each step then slowly folding in. Immobile he will look so like a dried blob of cut grass that one day I might crush him with the mower, then miss him dreadfully and feel a murderer for ever more, help, help!

Listen, we promise. During this legislation and the next, priority will go to the psychically under-privileged, we'll

51

declare a year for them, as for the handicapped, the children, the women, the eunuchs, the pack-animals and dogs. We promise to use all the diplomatic means at our disposal to transform individual aggressions into behaviour patterns that will be socially acceptable and politically agreeable to one and all.

For let there be no mistake, we shall find many of these second-class persons on the way, as many as there will be third-class persons, spokespersons, chairpersons, shadow ministers and undiplomatic sources close to shadow cabinets who will shadow-box and reveal then deny rumours, refuse to comment and sail round the world on polymonologues or run round non-aligned summits on record-breaking sprints, which will be a bit zigzaggy, making the future possible by achieving the anticipated in a new way, or doing more and more with less and less or less and less less and less well, we'll soon see which, with less and less freedom and more and more blackmail in the complicated psychology of all those who'll hate us still behaving as if. On verra ce qu'on verra and may the boast man whine.

Soon we shall have simulating machines for opinions, arguments, loves, hates, imaginings.

Wait. Hans will be coming any minute now.

Hans Who? I'll say.

No names idiot don't you know the rules? He'll bring the car into the garage. Now remember, not one move for ninety minutes after that. We'll have to be sure we won't be watched, that no late passer-by will turn up, no lights switch on in other houses. Only then shall we bring down the body and put it in the boot. Only tomorrow afternoon at three will you drive the car into town and leave it. You know your instructions? okay now keep quiet and go get some sleep, I'll wait for Hans.

That may be more convincing but for whom? The highway-person kidnapping a statesperson for instance then killing her off in cold blood for lack of direlogue or turning her into a wifperson which will come to much the same thing until she goes back to being a statesperson again? Or Andromeda may say it will be all very well and grand for him not to wish to pursue the subject after nevertheless pursuing his advantage with an evasive remark about repression being minimally necessary in any society, so let her put him right on this once and for all and Orion will proffersigh a digital disputer for instant resolution of stereotypes at the touch of a key so that one need not go through the whole process softwarily so many times, terror and counter-terror as a result of police brutality against non-violent demonstrations against war as terror against terror though she wouldn't admit for one moment that her very ability to argue this point and others without disappearing would tend to split her amalgam, but no, he'll simply be repeating propaganda, and as to the point he'll make so smugly about having well-off leftist friends and poor rightist ones it will fall flat with her, remember, she'll trace one side of her family back to Charlemagne and to practically all the ruling houses of Europe and she'll still be leftist and poor, well the latter will be relative, any admixture being possible, he should not think in categories.

Well!

As for my political beliefs, you should let them rest, and not lump me in with the dogmatic and intolerant.

And with this neat smash return of the amalgam ball into his court she will continue on her marathon way, the lack of political figures right or left whom one could trust won't lead her to the conclusion that one should abandon the ideas of justice, humanity or the good life, and he must allow her a mild preference in general for undesirable leftists over undesirable rightists without treating her as a raving political fanatic with a closed mind.

'Who would not be a good, kind person?' he will murmur dreamily, 'but circumstances would not have it so,' if I may quote a leftist if you must use these labels writer, Brecht.

Idiot, she'll exclaim meaning he'll give her the benefit Brecht. In any case criticism everywhere will soon be silenced for ever or forced underground, and the time won't be far off when you will be deprived of what, in a perfect some-of-my-best-friends argument, you yourself will go on calling your leftist friends, betraying your irritation, and you'll find yourself in the midst of an orderly but dismal bunch of rightists.

I shall look forward to the fulfilment of that virulent good wish, at any rate if you're right, for don't you see, Anna, that your argument must inevitably and each time lead to that of the terrorists, which will always be the daytaunt: arrest me, kill me, detain me without trial and you'll be no better than me. That will be the real dilemma of freedom from now on, and all the more so for the escalation of their methods, out of their very success, to state level. If I understand the real intent of that good wish it would be if I won't join you beat me, yes?

Oh come off it Orion, I really can't let you get away with that, which will for ever be the argument of privileged interest, like what will happen to Jews, Poles, and leftists won't matter much as long as one wouldn't happen to be one, important people will always identify with success, not with failure, won't they?

In what way could the left be called a failure? Or lacking in important people? In any case I should like to go over with you the curious sliding in your circular, repetitive disputation that somehow and each time must end up with your putting me, a leftwing Ukrainian out of Communist labour-camps which incidentally thousands of Poles and Jews will long remember, in with the privileged who by the same argument won't care what could happen to Jews, Poles and leftists?

Really Orion, why must you take every turn in the argument as personally applying to you, like a stupid woman? Why can't you keep the discussion abstract and impersonal?

Do you?

And he will touch her cheek gently with his broad hand as in movie farewells and maybe slide it down to press her shoulder and go. Garbage In, Garbage Out.

But Croesus will send his staffpersons to all the oracular sources, to Delphi, to Abas in Phocia, to Dodona, to Amphiarus and Trophonius, to Bracidae in Milesia. Not content with the Greek ones he will send also to the oracle of Ammon in Libya. His object will be to test their knowledge, so that if any should be in possession of the truth he might send a second time and ask if he should undertake a campaign against Cyrus. Only the spokesperson for Apollo at Delphi will pass the test.

Let me add however that if Hyperboreans exist beyond the north wind, there must also be Hypernotians beyond the south. From the North Foreland to Start Point the wind will be westerly force four and I shall go north to sweep the garbage of the gods exiled on a melting polarity, who will be waiting for the flood to submerge Time Squared and meanwhile watching from afar men kill the last young seals and last symbolic whales. They will look also at me, me and my broom, and say stay with us tall handsome Ethiopian man, longest lived and finest of all Libyan races, and sweep up the shit that we shall make, and when all the humans will have vanished from the face of the earth we shall give you a minor goddess, Ino for example —

Shit! I'll exclaim.

— but of course we would let you choose, and you will start mankind again ex almost nihilo as the return of the repressed prodigal, creating a new race.

Why?

Oh but there'll be no promethean forbidden fire this time no

55

pandoran curiosity and if there were she wouldn't be such a fool as to let it help men destroy themselves again.

Why should scientific curiosity be heroic in men and silly and mean in women? Your legends won't tempt me, even to be negated.

And there'll be no tree of knowledge of good and evil since all the trees and all the knowledge will have died, blasted by men who in their perpetual attempt to be as gods will have wrapped the planet in pure consciousness, innocently or wilfully ignorant of the fact that the consciousness of their gods will by definition be as impure as their own, stinking to high heaven.

Garbage In, Garbage Out.

But of course. You will understand everything. Your children and your children's children will conquer that earth once more but in tenderness and humility and they will be content with the created light. The secret of the uncreated light will be lost for ever and if it were found again the goddess ovules for ever transmitted through you will prevent men from knowing how to use it for good or ill, there'll be no push-button presidents and no push-button love, no warriors and no warrior's rests.

And all this out of your impure consciousness?

It may of course be too late. The Valkyries will be blinded by your modern wars and won't see any battlefields let alone battles to decide the issue of, any more than Athene will be capable of deciding anything with her Mentor exploded. Allah will will nothing, the Buddha won't budh nor will Raphael rhapsodize Adam on the knuckles. And who could be stupider than Jupiter?

So what?

Well, they'll go on tirelessly, you might as well stay with us and sweep the shit we can't help making, we'll always be anthropomorphic after all. If you gather it and lay it out over the ice-floe and pee on it regularly, snowdrops will grow, that will be a beginning. You will then take cuttings the following year, cross-pollinate them with the flowers we shall paint for you on the ice, transplant them in snow and potatoes will grow, the eyes of which you will gouge out and cross with fish eggs, just before the last fish die, and our goddesses will brood over them and you'll get a new race of performing seals. That should be enough to feed and protect you and your descendants without passing through the dinosaurs or even evolution, if at first we give you a little of our hydromel to keep you going, but you will have to calculate and watch the economy of your resources, grow more to live on than you destroy. Che sera sera and let the beast man wane.

He will not, I'll say, and I'll add let the boss man whine. You may go shiating on but as for me I shall refuse your weak white goddesses and your lack-lustre oblitopias without curiosity, I'll have no use for your god-shit, nor shall you ever be my gods nor my genies from plastic bottles nor my Hegelian moral imps.

But then, why come here?

To talk to you good god! Even sweeping up shit should be a form of communication you dismal bunch of rightists you face-saving devices you whited sepulchres. To tell you that the future of the world won't be kept back, or forth, but will be born, as before, in Africa, in the cradle of humanity and promised land when the milch and money of the West will have dried up and when your men the great of this world will have set their devastating fire to it as their crowing achievement, turned daytaunt to daybuckle and denounced themselves by their incurable warring greed, their indifference to our suffering and their diplomatic intrigues. Then we blacks shall bring home our ancestors in lumps of myrrh and repeople the promised land, we shall grow up as you grow down, we shall know how to work like slaves but willingly for ourselves, we shall sing our ancient gods you will have muzzled with your poppycockcrow, they'll be more earthy and more deeply powerful than you, and we shall wake them with our afrodizzyacts from their long sleep.

But listen, we promise.

57

Dearest nephew,

If you are coming by train you will have to take a taxi at the station, they will know the address. Tell me which train I'll order one for you, probably Mr Briggs, a delightful man. If you are coming by car you must continue on the main road after Godstone then turn left at Mark Cross. After about two miles you will come to a group of houses with a farm on the right, you'll see cows in the field, Jerseys. Turn right immediately after this farm into a lane winding upwards. You will reach my cottage (on the left at the top of the hill) after five minutes (just before the turning of the lane downwards along a wood). Could you possibly bring me some wholemeal country bread from town, we can't get it here. I trust you will not be bored with such a very wobbly lady. But come soon I may die any day. Much looking forward to your visit.

Your loving aunt,

Lizvieta.

Dear Mira Enketei,

I shall be coming over to England at the end of the month, would you like us to meet or not? If so please let me know. Meanwhile I will draw you a star from my belt for remembrance.

Love,

Orion.

P.S. Don't worry about the political quarrel. It will either be a mistake or emanations from your own thoughts.

Oh my prophetic soul my uncle ego, I Claudius as usual, stinking my sin to high heaven in a decoction of daughters and a broth of boys to be put through the softweird computer of immoral imps to reach, frankly, Charlemagne, Chuck Cherryblue Anne de Rommède Roland Fitzjohn Nelson Nwankwo and the rest. My Uncle Gigo will have done it all, spawning at will a race of performing souls sealed with neutralized Y or unneutralized X chromosomes or whirling dervish thoughts shaping up nebulae that will separate into worlds nations parties sects cells, the red and white globules of which will premutate in such a way as never to reproduce the same individual so that variation may clear the pipeline. Fathers and criminals will be identifiable with a margin of error of .0009 percent. I could take the ovule of a female say Andromeda, place it on a glass slide insert the drops from Orion's sword embed it in a highminded hypernotion and lo, after some premutations get Anna Biosis. Why bother however when I could pick Dolores Hans Jean-Luc Nelson or Chuck? I'll merely need more input. Which may be hard to select in the general flooding of the circuits.

The very complexity of the integrated systems would prevent them, in theory at any rate, from being fraudulently manipulated. On the other hand errors could easily be made. There must be a control of the codification at entry and a control of the results at exit, including the reprocessing of anomalies. If the necessary measures are not taken sufficiently early these terrors might not be spotted until very late. Garbage In, Garbage Out. Dear Uncle Gigo what shall I do? Will any of this still be there next time I look at it?

The prestidigital imputer for instance could marry Anne de Rommeda to Rinaldo Pozzi of Milano without leaving a trace on the genealogical tree, in order to account retroactively for the fact that the only women whose separate existence lovers will accept without a murmur at least for a while will be those belonging to others. Would the controller notice the fraudulent manipulation if the possibility weren't brought to his attention? And would he care, or would he shrug indifferently like

Orion, at so much irrelevant data clogging up the software?

Or shrug indifferently like Willy, at so much irrelevant flogging of dead horses as he will call my Pegasus wanderings that will also be clogging up the soft cheer.

None of my private telematics will interest him, why have private telematics he might as well say when you could have me and it would be a very good question while I'd think of an answer as to which would seem more fleshy and bloody among shadow figures, the electronic visitors speaking their colourful videolects like substitute guests and husbands blandly conversing in our livingrooms, or the twittering liewaypersons softwarily treading around the rotundity of a composite beast man waning fast and flat? The ghostly ingredients of all sexuality or the fleshpot itself? The simulacra on the wide screen in my spaceshipmind or the images Venus will abuse all lovers with already in Lucretius, you humanists, you intellectual snobs with your pretentious and obsolete culture he'll say and alas rightly why, you wouldn't even bother to understand the inside of car-bonnet. Then teach me, show me I'll say, instead of riposting about bothering to understand the inside of a psychic mechanism, but he'll prefer to keep car mysteries to himself, sliding off on to libwomen who'll nevertheless play pretty helpless on the road for some man to change a tyre. That would be how he'd like it to remain his smile at his own joke will say. Even in the supernew present technorevolution I could at best be the female slave who'll type the data into a memory for analysis but never, never the softquery expert who'll compose the analytic programme. I wouldn't understand.

Yet he'd probably like me now to have television in the farm kitchen to disguise the penultimate stage he won't admit, when from model-fatigue we'll have nothing to say even slightly in common except cuisine preferably haute and current affairs preferably general and through the distancing telescope of dismally bunched rightists. So I'll have to cook a great deal and upset my innards in rich restaurants and quote my lover substitute for him to comment on or drop him, but drop him he won't let me, he'll dismiss it as woman-nonsense and turn up again, and again. Soon I'll have as usual to behave real bad, flogging dead horses of truth to let him drop me as a scold. Neutral Cabinet sources will refuse to comment.

Meanwhile millions will die elsewhere, of disappearance in Argentine of appearances in Brazil of disappearance in Chile or vice versa, of guineaworms in Dahomey of fragmentation in Europe of finlandisation in Finland or vice versa, of settlement in Galilee of unsettlement in Honduras of relitigiousness in Iranireland of settlement in Jordan of unsettlement in Korea or vice versa, of terrorism in the Lebanon of repression in Mozambique of terrorism or freedom-fighting in Nicaragua or vice versa, of godlessness on Olympia of no ground in Palestine of little ground in Qatar or vice versa, of minority in Russia of majority in South Africa of democracy in Turkey of dictatorship in Uganda of democracy in Vietnam or vice versa, of counter-revolution in the Yemen of counter-counter-revolution in Zaïre and we'll all go on as if, so that the pipeline will be much cleared by your favourite Dan Daly the Man of Dawn, with you till six a.m. I want all you early birds and nightpersons truckdrivers bakers watchmen and insomniacs to phone in and tell me any funny stories you may know and in the second hour we'll play the number game right? Meanwhile we'll listen to some fabulous new songs okay?

Night will fade in and out of the soft dreamware worlds and diminishing cats and nightmare comments from our own correspondent on the bomb that will kill only people not their artefacts in a merely cool war, heat to be localized in an indecisive Europe and controlled since actions could only be tributaries of certitudes hello Mira?

Who could that be?

Orion. Get on with it will you or shut up your poppy-cockhead.

Oh I must thank you dear for the bread, and how are you, let me look at you she'll say, dear me I would never have recognized you, so thin, so tall. Please forgive, my emotion, be lenient towards a very old lady. Well now, I'll be forgetting

61

my manners next, come into the drawing-room dear. Sit down, sit down, I'll make some tea in a moment but tell me all about yourself.

I will he'll reply shyly, in due course, as it will occur, but I'd rather hear about you aunt Lizvieta.

Nonsense child she'll flutter if I started on my petty troubles, oh and joys too, joys too, you'd never be able to stop me in my old age. I want to hear all your news. But first I must get a small reproach out of the way, you will guess what you naughty boy. No? You want me to utter it? To reenact the accusation? Come come. But I'll forgive you of course, I couldn't expect to be the first attraction of your freedom but still, dear boy, why so long, I could have died.

But dear aunt Lizvieta, with no address to go by, you must know the complex workings of all administrations, even Red Cross inquiries.

She will look at him with the boundless love of a mother listening to her son's first lie.

You could do better than that my child but never mind, let's say no more, I'll light the samovar and fetch the tray. Yes dear, by all means, take the tray in, that would help me most, I might trip and fall and there would go all the best teaglasses and the china, flying to the floor with all the lovely goodies.

May I smoke?

What! Well of course you may, but not till after the goodies dear boy. And why take up such a nasty habit after fourteen years of enforced abstinence? Tell me dear, how do you live? What on? Ah, business. And what business? Sideburn ethics? Ah, computers. Well, well. And do you plan to remarry my dear?

No, I shall never remarry.

How can you be so sure? Have a biscuit.

Because, he'd say slowly between munches and sips, I'd always be having to choose between a woman who'd know me too well and one who'd never know me, between a woman who'd invent me in advance and one who'd forever live in the madlanes of memory she'd make hammeringly present.

Please explain. Would there be two women or one?

Two in a way, but one of them could only exist inside my mind, between my fear and my desire.

Always choose a woman who'll know you, even if too well, and teach her to conceal it. The other kind would be a dead loss to you, for ever rehashing old quarrels, like a state forever rewriting history.

He'll laugh. On that analogy aunt Lizvieta, a person living alone would be like a totalitarian state, with its only semblance of democracy an officialized self-criticism, while marriage would be the supposedly adult but more usually infantile rough and tumble of election campaigns and parliamentary debates.

Hmm. As to that my boy, perhaps a sound and simple religious grounding would teach you to berate yourself instead of the offender. But indeed you shouldn't live alone at your age, you'll become smug and self-satisfied.

So marriage to you would really be a daily calling into question?

And reaffirmation, both of course.

Well. Such a choice would be rather hypothetical.

But why?

Most people will accept in theory but not take in practice a daily calling into question.

I wouldn't dream of seeing you marrying most people my dear she'll answer with a wicked bright blue glint.

The highest marks will go not to the most correct but to the most ingenious. Let a and b stand for mutually exclusive hypotheses, extrapolate to x.

Have another biscuit dear, help yourself. Tell me about my sister.

There'll be a pause and he'll gulp down a mouthful of tea. I can't, he'll say at last.

What!

Oh, aunt Lizvieta, please forgive me for springing it like this without previous warning, but try to understand. If it were given to me to make that, choice, again, either to leave with-

63

out seeing my mother, ever again, or to see her and stay, but in a state asylum I, forgive me, I can't, speak, of it.

More tea?

More recipes, more planting instructions, more forecasts of certain economic growth of neuroses that like animals will have to be fed, more ultimate prophecies beyond which logically could loom only the void Mira?

Er — Orion?

Yes, don't you know my voice by now? Tell me, do you want to see me or not?

Well I'll say, hesitating, no, I'd rather not.

Oh? He'll sound surprised. Why not?

I suppose it might confuse me — but that'll sound lame — or tire me, or bore me, or alarm me.

And you can't decide which? This will be said ironically.

No, oddly enough in your view I expect and his tone will in fact decide me, but I wouldn't be prepared to risk it.

There'll be one of those pauses.

Could you be, well, he'll say, annoyed?

At what, Orion? I'll ask, knowing full well.

At the competition perhaps?

I'll gently press the cut-off button.

So why in the name of all creation can't I do that with Willy?

Perhaps because there wouldn't be a phone at the farm?

And then Croesus, with food for second thoughts from the increasing power of Cyrus, will test the oracles, telling each of his staffpersons to go and consult each oracle in exactly a hundred days and inquire what Croesus will be doing at that moment. And who but Apollo through the spokesperson at Delphi will imagine that Croesus, carefully keeping to the agreed date, would go to the beach and with his own hands cut up a tortoise and a lamb and boil them together in a bronze cauldron with a bronze lid? Shall I advance or retreat, he'll ask later. Yes. Yes what? Yes Your Majesty. Oh come off it Apollo be vocal not equivocal. Well Your Majesty, if you attack Persia you will destroy a great empire. Afterwards, with bitterness and a kind of wisdom he will learn pre-suppositional logic and the transgressed rules of coreference deleted but recoverable by schools of afterthought.

Meanwhile things will continue to be mildly pressurable, even sexasperating. Nor will he ever know how instead of dinenwining up vaguely diffuse desire out of kind cowardice I could at the drop of a batting eyelid be so much more real, disputing about politics in other words love with Orion or skeletally digesting my rodent hunger and longing daily for Mussa to return from the hills. He will not return, he will be killed in this horrible and endless war and I shall never feel his eyes burning my black breasts his gentle fingers on my neck or down along my body into my sex as I shall for ever imagine. Instead I shall be nearing twenty and old, my breasts will surely sag my belly will be swollen with hunger and my bones will stick out and Mustapha will return and roughly take me, even without camels. I shall bear him children and obey him in

65

all things, dreaming of my poet Mussa. And Mustapha will go back to the war and my sons will grow up and go to the war. Slowly perhaps the image of my lost poet will fade a little at the edges like an aura and become less painful. Fatima my folly my fair one he will still sing in my head how like a bark your body how it will race down my rivers, cradling my body, Fatima my folly how could such rivers run in a dry land? The cradling bark will create rivers for ever as two ivory tusks will create the elephant between them.

> An wenna wanna scream ahl scream, see!
> An wenna wanna dream ahl dream, free!
> An wenna wanna luv ahl luv, you!
> An wenna wanna shuv ahl shuv, shoo!
> An wenna wanna ride ahl ride, high!
> An wenna wanna hide ahl hide, bye!
> An wenna wanna dip ahl strip, out!
> An wenna wanna trip ahl flip, out!
> An wenna wanna die ahl die, too
> An wenna wanna die ahl die (bis till fade out)

Great, Chuck, Dave will shout, that'll be a hit, another crazy hit, you'll see.

Oh shucks, I'll mutter d'you really think so?

Top of the charts for weeks, mark my words.

An I sure gonna need it I'll go on muttering angrily.

Quit worrying Chuck he'll say and that'll be what I'll want, you'll be up that ladder in no time and stay there.

Yeah, but, well, I sure gonna need it.

Don't live it up so he'll say bang on cue.

Live it up! I'll say bang on cue how can I Dave, with that damn dame claiming alimoney an her ole man behind her pontificatering about damage to repute an standards to which an all, as if it wouldn't all go to save the sodding ole stately home.

Oh come off it Chuck, he may be a British gent after all or the judge'll be on your side.

Judges won't take sides, not in England anyways.

Course they will, what, jes for a coupla years together —
Well more

For a coupla years an a bit you'd be dishing out for ever, paying for not fucking the dame? That may be our law here but not in little ole England, anyways they'd have their poorman's pride an honor of aristos wouldn't they?

You don't know the dame my lady Caroline an all.

Well, take that predge when you come to it Chuck, meanwhile sing away and quit worrying. Let's run through it again shall we?

Okay Hans, I'll say. Roberto'll drive the Renault into town tomorrow at three p.m. You'll leave here at six a.m. in the Volkswagen and go north to Point Z. Meanwhile we must burn these documents and pack the typewriter into the boot and we should do it soon.

Which boot? he'll ask sharp as a knife.

Well the Volkswagen of course not the Renault the body'll be in that.

Okay, go on.

I'll look at him wishing he wouldn't take himself quite so seriously as a filmbullyboss. Then I'll repeat my lesson.

You'll deposit the typewriter at Point Q on the way. At eleven I'll leave on foot with Gisela, taking the note. We'll lock up, Gisela will pocket the key, we'll take the bus together to Point 42, here, I'll say pointing on the map, then separate. Gisela will go by bus to Tottenham Court Road, walk towards Holborn and meet Sean at Henekey's where she'll give him the key. I'll go by tube to Charing Cross, have lunch slowly, go to Point 6 and change, wait, then I'll walk to Point 1, see the Renault, walk to Point 12 and phone the Mail —

No.

Right, I'll first leave the note in the rubbish bin at Point 11, then walk to Point 12 and phone the Mail, then back to Point 6, where I'll change again, then walk across the bridge to Waterloo Station and take the train to Point L. Gisela will have left town by then and will join you at Point Z, zigzagging via Colchester and Cambridge.

And Roberto?

Oh yes. He'll park the car at Point 1 and walk, at normal pace, looking at shops, to St Paul's, where he'll take the bus to Point 28. Abdel will drive him out of town well before I shall leave the note, to Point N where he'll lie low with Susumu. Abdel will return to Point 28.

Will he be all right? Hans will ask.

Abdel?

No, Roberto.

Sure I'll say loyally.

I'd prefer to do that part myself and have him do mine.

He'll be okay, Hans, and totally unknown. You must respect democratic decisions and trust him, it'll be the making of him.

It may be the unmaking of us, Alexei. The risk'll be great and at the crucial stage we shouldn't be thinking of boosting the ego of relatively new recruits.

We must think of the future, Hans, and train the coming generations, it'll be a long struggle.

Maybe. But if anything should go wrong with that bit —

Nothing'll go wrong, Hans, he'll be well prepared and very calm. And if anything should go wrong, what could happen at worst? They'd corner him, find the body too soon, he'd be arrested.

And what if he panicked, tried to run for it or shoot it out, they'd shoot him down.

So what? There'll always be sacrifices I'll say toughly, shrugging my shoulders, and in any case it'll be too late, the body in the boot will speak for itself.

And if they don't kill him but get him he might be the one to speak.

Nonsense, look at the others. He wouldn't dare, with that example.

Well if this turns out to be an error of judgement Alexei you'll pay for it. We can't afford errors at any stage.

Okay I'll pay for it, but I'll stake my head on success.

Not your head Alexei, we'll need it and you'll always know

68

that.

Arsa eerah sa eerah sa eerah! How does it go Dave, something about hanging aristos, gee I might make a hard rock hit
with that, listen . . . But you'd have to adapt the words.

It sure wouldn't kinduv inspire me. And you should guard
your image too.

What image?

Oh come on Chuck, you'll always be sociated with that
marrying a dook's daughter.

Earl.

They'll be calling you Dook Cherryblue. You can't have
your duke and hang him. An people'd think yer'd be full of
kidstuff revenge.

Say howbout an alimoney lament? Something about
women's lib like as long as they'll go on selling theirselves in an
out of marriage an getting bread for not sleeping with a guy
they'll always be dunned as objects, right? Well yer'd put it
better ercourse, with rhymes an rhythm an all.

We should wait, Chuck, an see how things'll turn out.

Okay but no harm in working on it, to exploit the boilin'
blood?

Your blood Chuck, mine ain't boiling why don't you have a
go? I wouldntuv gotten into that mess in the first place.

Quit preachin will yer.

Could love as game, as open-eyed choice of will and not of
need be also a woman's prerogative?

India. A particularly long pre-monsoon period may cause
serious famine. According to a government spokesman in
New Delhi his country will appeal to the United Nations for
extra support. The greater part of Asia will be discovered by
Darius, who will follow the Indus eastward to the sea, thus
proving that Asia too, except for the easterly part, of which we
don't know anything, must be surrounded by sea and bear a
general geographic resemblance to Libya. The people of the
Pacific, with their strong business sense their willingness to
work their nimble electronic fingers will cause the centre of
wealth in the twentyfirst century to shift from one ocean to

another. Both Atlantic capitalism and Asian State capitalism may crumble from inside. Cricket. But then to Herodotus the world would have the exact shape of the human brain, with water on it for mare internum, and water around it as yet unexplored.

And in every human brain millions of bits of information that would fit millions of books my lover substitute will by then be saying let alone oral tradition that will circulate more or less available at any one chosen moment owing to the dispersal of the memory files such as hello, head-hunter?

Yes? I'll confirm and query cautiously.

Shut up will you.

What do you mean?

What a lowdown trick, so my lady would be bored would she, or tired, or confused to see me, then behind my back ever so vicariously have her fun?

Orion, stop shadow-boxing me with your boring political quarrel do you think I'd care about boosting and busting egos dressing up in dialectics when the world —

The world's ego won't be any different Mira my girl meanwhile you won't imprison me in your forgetfulness to be now made present by my existence, why can't you argue the damn thing out logically and honestly?

And why, Orion, can't you remember your aunt's advice and berate yourself instead of the offender?

And how do you know I don't as well?

As well, yes, but not instead of.

Stick to the point and stop amusing yourself at our expense.

But yes he will be jealous and I shall stupidly be pleased. Orion, simmer down I'll say maternally like Willy saying paternally I mustn't worry, you should be pleased that I should free you in this way, why, a neurotic discourse will always win by dragging the other's down into itself if you let it.

So?

So just keep silent, now you can go back to the future and other negative capabilities.

Be careful Mira, don't go too far or I'll step right out, he'll use the usual blackmail, you of all people should also recall my aunt's advice and even apply it, for you'll only be displacing your own berating to more distant and ideal levels, all part of yourself, remember?

That'll be unfair but touché. All right all right I'll say, ignore it, forget it.

So I will but cut it out and bring me back and stop your swinegirl warnings.

Calm down Orion, do you think it easy with so much violence all around and ahead and pigs to raise and a man who

They will fly away.

Will they? Can pigs have wings?

See you later world berater.

When in nomansland do as nomans will. Instead of not as well as, as well as not instead of, but the first will project on to the second for any communication worth while or even not, such as when more or less kindly more or less directly I'll be pouring another break-feast attempt into Willy's ears and with incredulity hear them click shut again in favour of the studied zeal he'll use to hear the air-filling trivia, excuse me he'll say during the tap-runnings and such could you repeat? And when

71

I shall have left him it will remain a mystery to me whether anyone so physically solid would always and for others seem to lack a whole dimension of being or will it be only for me, my own dimension I won't have given him?

We'll take that project when we'll come to it, will that always be your attitude in the West Mr Lagerkvist, my lover substitute will say, let's call him Nelson Nwankwo, smoothly, holding his cocktail glass. The Swede will give him the diplomatic gaze, staring first at him then beyond and around as if addressing his diplomatic silences to the world at large through him.

We shall indeed, take that dodge when and if it should become a serious threat. Come, Dr Nwankwo, the role of the voice in the wilderness couldn't be less appropriate, we shall always be several technological steps ahead of catastrophe.

Technological steps perhaps, Nelson will reply, not easily controlling his outrage at this invisibility treatment, but when will the morally dedeveloping countries start morally developing at the same pace? What could be the point of creating so many international organizations producing report after report if governments will continue to file them away and do nothing.

Nothing? The Swede will refocus with a bored effort. Come, do not exaggerate.

Zero point thirty-three percent, dropping to zero point thirty, of their joint GNP, small countries like Sweden and Norway incidentally contributing the highest percentage of theirs, the big powers the lowest, except of course for armament. A few face-saving devices.

Wouldn't you be confusing, Lagerkvist will drawl, two separate lots of statistics, quoting the percentage of the budget in the one case and of the GNP in the other?

Well er, there'll be a split second of panic, if you know the figures it wouldn't affect the general argument. Millions of children of the globe whose brains may atrophy for lack of protein, a ninety percent illiteracy when you must know that no modern civilization can progress at over fifty percent. Thus you will continue to be comfortably convinced of our inferiority, while the reports will continue to prove that stabilizing of population may only occur with a decent standard of living. You will —

On the contrary sir, we'll continue, as ever, to do our best, but you shouldn't underestimate the difficulties. The so-called rich countries will go on making vast loans to those of the third world —

At superhigh interests, which will increase with every debt consolidation, each time to be carefully rescheduled and premeditated, risking, for mounting profits, the world's whole banking system which in its collapse would plunge the people of all nations but especially the poor into the deepest misery. Will those always be your moral imperatives?

Kindly do not interrupt me, my dear sir. We'll pour in money, much of it will get deflected as usual into the pockets of your rulers and their advisers, not to mention everyone taking his cut all the way down the line. We'll continue to build roads, bridges, barrages, factories, mining enterprises, pipelines, schools, hospitals, and your rulers will continue to choose the showy and useless instead of the designs we'll spend much time and money in studying for your needs and climate, and they'll continue to prefabricate underdevelopment from birth onwards by insisting on retaining native traditions that'll be good enough for the vast majority of the poor but not of course for them with their European educations and their palatial villas.

And the dawn will end and I shall rise to feed the man and then the pigs or vice versa and talk in a friendly way to one and all, will that little one survive? See here Connecticut, only connect, fight your way to the tits, way up that vast pink wall, see? There, don't let yourself be ousted by your brothers of milk and tummy, squeak up, loud and clear, off Idaho you swine, now shoo, let him have a tit too don't hog it you selfish pig you power maniac.

Good morning folks now have you any recipes or useful household hints to give your fellow listeners please ring between nine and eleven to impart your knowledge to one and all, but first we'll listen to some smashing records Tennessee stop it and you too Washington get off that tit, okay squeak away but he'll stay much smaller at this rate you should be ashamed of yourselves, in any case it won't do you the slightest bit of good, you'll merely be ready for the butcher sooner, do you think I could afford to be sentimental merely on account of names? Let us recognize one another before annihilating each other, why, we'll be having an explosive topic for discussion today with if I may say so an explosive but charming lady I'll introduce you to in a moment. The question today will be do you prefer twin beds or singles, ring up and tell us your views your experiences and be patient girls the exchange will get superblocked so just keep trying and they will, they will, all day, to question the hired cyberneticians of hunger the geophysicists of fear the economists of injustice the demographers of desire the psychoengineers of violence the technogymnasts of politics the mythopathologists of jour-nalism the ethnologists of revolution the vulcanologists of diplomacy the ecologists of information the oecumenologists of nostalgia who will tell you what to think of it all and interchangeable until Perry Hupsos and his late night show to be followed by Dial Dolores hello? If you attack the Persians O Croesus, you will destroy a great empire. Croesus, overjoyed, will name his shadow cabinet send gifts of gold to Delphi and prepare to destroy the power of Cyrus.

Swing low Iscariot. Soon the earth will wrap itself in its poisonous discourse of which government spokespersons will deny the rumour, speaking softly to its nervous system, in-flate, recess, water copiously and it will loveinbloom as a poppycockcrow. This may well be my crowning achievement after all. Take a human hair, split it in four, whip it up with the whites of their eyes, rehandle thoroughly with fresh modifiers finely chopped and pour into a battered wish, bake in a moderate speech for twenty minutes. Temperatures will drop to the right of the country, with frowns and intermittent wails but smiling patches here and there in the home counties. To the left of the country the temperatures will rise quite high with threat of storms and localized gnashing of teeth. Towards the south-west, the furthest inhabited land would seem to be Ethiopia in Libya, full of gold, huge elephants, ebony, wild growing trees and the tallest men in the world who may well be the best looking too and the longest lived. As for Europe, shall we ever make it, will it be green or red or black and blue?

But then, in forty-five million years the Red Sea will be an ocean separating Africa from Asia while America will collide with China hello Dolores? And who could that be? Marian? And what do you want to talk about Marian something gay something sad something that may be troubling you? Well I don't know how to start. Don't be afraid Marian I won't eat you nor will the listeners in our big chain of friendship, perhaps you will find someone who'll want to help you. Well you see Dolores my husband. Yes? They will obey and call, all night and day, out of solitude despair need to show off to search for supersolidarity or by way of small ads in the name of participation, saving millions in professional airtime, and when the programmes change they'll readapt and go on ringing dutifully about bathtubs delphiniums fringe medicine or benefits the Gaza strip artificial colouring race relations abortion football drag treeplanting you name it they will respond and ring, aren't you all marvellous and I'll rather agree, I'll be fascinated what tripe, Willy will say, a pseudo-democracy an opium of the people. Our industrial corre-spondent our financial correspondent our correspondent in Berlin Buenos Aires Beirut Bonn Brussels Budapest Bucharest Belgrade Baghdad Bogota will be in touch with us in a few minutes and tell us what to think of it.

You'll have to see further than that Mr Lagerkvist. Can't you understand that a few drops in the desert, deceptive drops from which you'll extract sweat and blood to serve your interests, won't solve anything but merely breed more misery, confusion, violence, guerilla warfare, terrorism with eventual home-made atom bombs? What will your technological know-how do against that, waning as it will in any case with

75

your population, the latter producing more future terrorists than technicians, thanks to disastrous educational and economic policies, all your kids who won't get work, who'll opt out of your system, do you think death and decline won't happen to you, will be for others only?

Allow me to suggest, doctor, that you may be misinterpreting the symptoms. Opting out would seem to be, rather, a phenomenon of economic boom, the kids wouldn't afford it in economic crisis.

Ah, so unemployment should ideally be maintained, the old capitalist argument, to keep everyone obedient. But you know that won't work, just look around you Dolores?

Hello? Who's that?

Tom, the voice will say, or Dick or Homer.

And what would you like to talk about Homer?

I'd like to tell you about plural sex. If it doesn't shock you.

Why should I be shocked Homer? Though I'd be curious to know, would it be me you'd want to shock or the world?

There'll be a slight pause.

Well it could interest other listeners couldn't it?

It could indeed, go ahead then.

Well, and into the night, saving millions in royalties by tapping vicarious polypredispositions under the guise of listener participation. But mark my words Dr Nwankwo will insist, do not close your eyes to the Third or even the Fourth world, for your own sakes, act on the experts' reports instead of shillyshallying from conference to conference. You may well think, secretly or half-consciously, that with our expectation of life no higher than in your Middle Ages, or with enough natural and health catastrophes equivalent to your Great Plague, the situation will balance out and you will be protected, hence your minimal efforts under much lipservice to save the starving. Can't you learn even the lessons of your own history, that violence will always be stronger in the long run, than famine and disaster, because of famine and disaster? Must you for ever export your Middle Ages, letting the neosub Gandhis of our world proclaim that in order to protect

76

their non-violence they will have a national defence, just like you, taking it from this or that side, which will be merely practising their future wars not to mention that of outer space?

My dear Dr Nwankwo, must you amalgamate so many complex issues in your tireless flow? Our awareness will increase daily, more than you may think, as will the thousands of highly competent experts working on these problems everywhere and —

Oh yes my friend, you may have the competent people, you may hold the key to the future, but you will not give it to us.

We shall, my friend, we shall, and may I thank you for calling me your friend. But as a friend I would advise you not to mix up so many tired generalizations in your speech to the assembly, but to stick to concrete proposals. The role of Cassandra will hardly suit you and will hardly help. Let's be more optimistic, we could be at the trough of the wave, let's believe in man.

Let's believe in man the father almighty, and in his only son genius nice, out of a plastic bottle, the eternal return of the repressed prodigy. Let us not be surprised if with the army of Xerxes consisting in all of 5,283,320 men, the rivers should sometimes fail to provide enough water. But the food won't give out for if the daily ration for one man be kept to a quart of meal, the total daily consumption would be 110,340 bushels, not of course counting women, eunuchs, pack-horses and dogs.

None will be prophets on their own planet.

But will it always be the fate of seers to utter idées by definition reçues from everysomewhere suspended in some black cloud of news enveloping the earth and ever replenished, at which kings and counsellors will shrug and talk of wave troughs silver linings bright tunnel-ends and chrome eldorados for all? The clichés of the future will develop however, framed in a big surprise as value added such as dynamic structures for instance that will change while passing through the minds of their observers, seers, readers, cyberneticians, historians, pig-farmers and such.

Thus Professor Albireo Cygnus will lecture tomorrow in a big hall and deny the rumours that the sign could be about to collapse, although any one system possessing, from a prag-matic point of view, great modelling power, may in a latter phase come to seem a set of signs without denotata, like for example the semiotic system of fortune-telling which in ancient cultures might so influence the decisions of rulers. Prohibitions indeed may become injunctions and alter a semiotic system, look for example at the mediaeval, biblical and even aristotelian prohibition of usury, after the history and description of which a group of students will suddenly march out and invade The World Bank, plagiarizing a very important perception by taking a very important statesperson as hostage, an event which will open wide the black hole of international finance wherein tottering budgets huge fortunes told and un-told will be engulfed like sardines in a whale.

Thus far there will have been nothing worse than person-stealing on both sides but as for what will happen next the semiotic system will crash the wall streets of the cities will swarm with the dark passions and black panics of small savers high gamblers and tall banktellers of tales.

Meanwhile all frontier posts will be watched by Extrapol, road blocks will be set up everywhere and all cars searched by international verifiers. Stunned sources close to financial sources will reveal what police sources will refuse to comment, shadow cabinets will shadowbox with ghost writers of sources close to the treasury and spokespersons of secret city sources will persistently deny persistent rumours from the huge headlines and the breastbeatings under which truth will be arraigned as traitor to reality. Then they will launch a great dehauntological campaign. Sociopsychideologists from all over the world will measure the breastbeatings and calculate their agnostications and tell us what to think of it.

Down at the crumbling farm, I shall be surprised to tread almost on the dead toad's baby son, he'll be as small as a coin and as camouflaged on the moonlit gravel. Forgive me little one I'll look out for you now till you grow big and prehistoric like your father, but you look out too, I don't want to be a patricide again, get back under the hydrangeas.

Stop talking to yourself Mira, get on with your job, go feed the prisoner.

How, I'll ask, she won't eat.

Talk to her, force her.

That should be Gisela's job. When will Hans arrive?

Mind your own business.

May I remind you Roberto that if you use my house in this high-handed way you might at least observe the rules of elementary courtesy and allow me to get on with —

Courtesy shit, we'll observe our own rules, least knowledge least betrayal and get on with your orders.

I would think that efficiency, let alone democracy, would require everyone concerned to know as —

Oh shut up will you. And close the damn shutters.

I must see to the new litter.

Shut your trap schoolmarm.

I would seem to be unpopular with these characters. Will every litter each time contain two piglets who never get to the teat in time, like Connecticut, and now Wisconsin and Utah, who'll wait for the others to finish and crawl timidly forward, getting only the dregs? Smaller, thinner, weaker, they'll never catch up. Come on, Wisco, get to it now, look, up there, the big fat one. Silly slob, don't be frightened of my hands they're gonna help you. There, see? Next time get their first, or stick around it, use your pigwits if you're weaker, don't you have any? No? Well it's gonna be tough for you then. But using more and more artificial energy if I may say so my lover substitute will say so, as it were atomic for anatomic, not for instance that of horses, oxen, women and — ah, so you'd put women in with the oxen would you? Er not at all madam, you should let me finish my sentence, and so the experts and sado-experts will rumble on, leaning over the rumbling world and muttering smoothing prognostications and we'll all go on as if, half an ear on the lover substitute and half on the anatomic energy of pigsqueaks and snorts and grunts with working hours, nineteen miles, falling slowly, good, becoming moderate, purchasing power, falling more quickly, productivity sixteen miles, rising slowly, visibility poor, rain later, becoming moderate or fair, unemployment four million, steady, then moderate with fog patches becoming fair, leisure hours rising, soon, until hello, Dolores?

Hello, who would that be?

Charlie.

And what will you talk to me about Charlie?

Well I'd like to know what you'd think of the kidnapping.

That would be a little outside the scope of this programme Charlie, there'll be experts commenting again in the morning to tell you what to think of it, why don't you talk to me about yourself, what do you do in life?

Do we have to have this on?

Yes, till Hans brings the special. What could be keeping him?

Shshsh, that'll be him, open up.

Hi, Hans.

Hi, gimme some food will you, hey, what the hell, my big sister.

80

Your sister?

Our Lady of Sorrows, yep, Dolores.

But Hans, no names, remember.

So what, my dear cousin Mira here will already know my name won't she? Shit, why this toy radio anyway?

But Hans, don't you have the big stuff with you?

Idiot Roberto, do you suppose I'd drive around with that gear in my car? Go look in the pigstable.

Do you mean that big case, oh lord, how could I know?

Ow loord, hauw could I knouw! Go help her with it Roberto. Wait, listen — from our news desk.

A silence will follow then a buzz kidnappers. Doctors' warning to the kidnappers. Doctors' warning to the kidnappers. The prisoner cannot take normal, food, repeat, the prisoner cannot take normal food. The prisoner will die unless fed exclusively on capital. The prisoner will die unless fed exclusively on capital.

I'll have to resign as hostess then, I don't have capital.

Find some.

What me? How? That should be your job, go hold up a bank, or several, a little at a time would do.

How dumb can you get? They'd guess and watch out for us, could even be a trap. No. We'll have to appeal to our own people, just in case, though we'll go on trying her on food meanwhile.

She won't touch it.

Stop interrupting Mira. Listen Roberto, I must get some sleep. Take the car, no door-slamming mind, they'll click quietly. Go silent and slow at first, then at moderate speed to Point X. Try and make it before dawn, and take country roads, here, study the roadblocks first, memorize'm. At X Sean will help you out, lie low for twenty-four hours then come back the long way, at a leisurely pace, in daylight. Put the bread in the second false bottom. And tell'm to organize some more for when we get to Point Y.

When will that be?

Mira will you shut up. Roberto get a move on.

81

Okay Hans. But shouldn't we just let her die, won't this be an unneccesary risk? We intend to kill her, not to bargain, and wouldn't her death be the point of it all? What could they give us in exchange? The prisoners, you'll say, but afterwards? They'd merely start using her again. Even they won't regard it as an ordinary hostage affair, and morally speaking —

Cut your morally speaking, shall I always be surrounded with half-wits? We must keep her alive as long as possible, not to give her back but to raise their hopes with proofs of life and create chaos towards a new society, otherwise they'll start adjusting more drastically do I have to explain everything now get on with it I must sleep. You Mira listen to the police messages and wake me up should there be anything.

Please, couldn't Gisela?

She wouldn't understand fast enough.

But she would, Hans, I'll explain the code it'll be very repetitive. I'll need sleep too. Don't forget my job as cover and hostess, shopping for my cousin and his friends on holiday, biking to the village, cooking, behaving normally gardening pigfeeding and all that.

Fair enough, go wake her. But there'll be no biking to the village for you my girl, she'll go or I'll go.

Now why should I be in this bizarre situation could I be in love with cousin Hans? Or with my thesis-superviser Cygnans/Signatum who could be signing the action like a sort of Uncle Gigo? Shall I in the huge small hours sleep as an engine hurtling into the black and endless void or dream of the diminishing cat unfed and fatally developing to a foetal dedevelopment, to be spawned on a lonely shore in noman's promised land and write in a helpless wriggle of forming fins its cybernetic story on the sand and away? Shall I crawl montecristoid through prison walls and dive by air land or sea if so I must instruct all X and Y chromosomes within me to make the future possible or to hold it back, or forth. Let sex equal why.

Soon the prophecies will come out of input as Garbage In, and we shall all become oracular computers, Draculas sucking endless information from the napetrough of a wavelength, murders holdups wars natural catastrophes coodaytahs space-launches daytaunts cultural items and sportspersons sailing round the world on an analogue. The very foetus will be programmed into a prophetus curling up in the womb with a book of genetic information and occasionally switching on or off the booming disco of his mother's fears and tantrums and galloping vote inventions right left of centre. Vote for us now and at the hour of our birth, when we shall have to carry our dead parent with us in a lump of myrrh through the amalgamuddle to the ultimate foreknowledge which being ultimate will have to be knowledge of nothing at all. The sibyl will be sibling to the electronic game that will teach kids to count on nothing write on silicon and read off. Listen, I promise that the Persian booty will be divided amongst the troops, each man receiving his due. But I Pausanias as commanding general will if victorious have a right to ten of everything, women, horses, camels, gold pieces and other objects.

Dear Uncle Ego,
What will you do with aunt Lizvieta, Orion, Andromeda and Willy, with Fatima and Mussa, Chuck Cherryblue and Erik Lagerkvist and Dr Nwankwo and Hans and Co? I would advise you to be reasonable and yield up your hostages at once. The acting government will not give in to your demands, nor will the shadow-acting one.

Your alter ego, Gigo

What come to that will he demand? Not milch nor money, only a plane of vision to fly away from me to the other obscene, where he will be well treated and set free, the expectoration generating the expected pleasure of recognition.
Meanwhile the negoshiating will attempt to go shiating on in the void of radio time through Nat the Nightman and Dan the Man of Dawn. A Zurich gnome will arrive to shadowact as

mediator. But how mediate with silent kidnappers?

Please, don't, switch, off.

Come again?

Let me, listen, to him.

Aha. Well if you're a good girl and eat we'll let you listen.

Can't. Message, truth, gnome, please.

Glory be. Such a grand top lady statesperson and in love with a gnome?

Please. Gnome, will, substitute. For capital. For, food.

Well! . . . Say, Gisela, can you take over a minute?

Warum?

I must go down and have a word with Hans?

Vy? You love him?

Don't be silly. Business, urgent. Only a minute, please.

Ach. Okay.

I'll pay it back, Gisela. Hans! Hans? Ah, Hans, what do you know! The prisoner will derive sustenance in abstract form.

Talk normal will you.

Well apparently if she could listen to the Zurich gnome it would be like capital, or next best.

You mean that? Shit let's check. Say, that'd be a great idea! We could substitute.

Substitute for a gnome, himself a substitute for capital, itself a substitute for food? How?

With a giant.

Could *you* talk normal? Or do you mean Hegelian moral imps?

D'you have a copy of *Das Kapital* here? Abridged? Okay fetch it. You'll have to prepare it a bit we must introduce it in small slices and start with the most technical, less violent parts. But if she's hungry she'll absorb it all.

You must be joking! D'you mean I'll have to read aloud to her? From Karl Marx?

Only twice a day, for half an hour.

But, but, what about my work, my pigs, my vegetables, my, oh and how can I prepare something I don't really know or fully understand? And for an expert too!

84

Crap, statespersons wouldn't be, they'd have experts. And Gisela'll prepare it, she'll even share in the reading.

But the prisoner won't understand with Gisela's accent, and she won't take it anyway from a woman's voice, she'll be used to manhandling male statespersons around her, she'll need a deep high-financial voice.

Why such prejudice from you? Well, maybe. I'll start then, I'll make the transition from the radio-gnome. But very little at first in fact, five or ten minutes, we must keep her craving. Then she won't notice the change of voice. Slowly we'll step up the dose. By the time we'll use the Geryon and cancer bits and all that she'll be indoctrinated. Meanwhile let her have the radio, but only for the gnome mind you, no monetary or other news.

Thus the gnome of Zurich will be transmuted from a radio-gnome through an astrognome with millions of astronoughts into the giant of Trier. Their vectors will intersect in zig-zagging disjunctions exclusive and inclusive. The first point of intersection will be the word of honour lost in mounting interest, the second infinite need with no ground to stand on, the third the crisis, recessing in unwanted works, the fourth the crash, lost in infinite regressions towards a promised land of ilk and money as computered by the dirthly paradigm.

Swing low, Iscariot, enter the judas lens and speak to an issue with a tissue of lies. Allegiances will be lifted, greetings will be declared closed till the next balance shit, turning the other cheek to cheek till the next unloading of yellow terror from the underbellies of monsters in the sky disguised as ideologies. Where e'er you'll walk my broom shall dog your anal infrastructures.

And then I shall walk in with my hypotheses, like let sex equal why or once upon a spacetime there could be a beautiful princess with evasive eyes, who would be called Fatima my Folly. She will live in a beautiful castle the Castle of Point X, overseeing the white city of Point X.

The citizens of Point X will be very happy to go about their multiplex business dividing and subdividing and singing the praises of their princess Fatima my Folly and of course those of her father the old king, Carolus Magnus. Beyond the walls of the city the peasants will tractotill the intractable tracts of soil that will be frequently scorched by the ravages of a distant neighbour the Dragon whose periodic touristic expeditions will wrap the land in his shortwinded bad breath and cost a heavy tribute. Beyond the fields, forests of paper will burn and be patiently replanted with press cuttings to supply the city with newsprint for its daily sensations.

One day the Princess Fatima my Folly will take her late morning walk along the battlements, to the cheers of the local population. And on that very one day the Dragon, holding his bad breath and avoiding his usual route over the forests and fields, will inevitably but unexpectedly appear round the mountain behind the castle, and in the long curl of his tail seize the princess whose evasive eyes will miss his sudden approach and he'll fly off with her. His action will be so swift and silent that the castle cannons will not even manage to alter their normal downward overseeing aim to erections fast enough.

The old king will tear at his long flowery beard, the land will be plunged in official mourning and despair. The old king will then issue a proclamation.

Oyez oyez the proclamation of His Most Exalted and Most Beloved Majesty Carolus Magnus King of Point X, will call out the Royal Herald on Frequency Modulation. Article 1. We Most Exalted and Most Beloved Majesty King Carolus Magnus King of Point X shall hereby give the hand of Our only daughter Her Royal Highness the Princess Fatima my Folly to any man who will succeed in rescuing Her Royal Highness the Princess Fatima my Folly alive from the claws of the Dragon, Terrible and Traditional Enemy of the Kingdom of Point X. Article 2. We Most Exalted and Most Beloved Majesty King Carolus Magnus King of Point X will hereby also hand over the inheritance of Our Kingdom to any man who will succeed, while saving Her Royal Highness the Princess Fatima my Folly alive from the claws of the Dragon, Terrible and Traditional Enemy of the Kingdom of Point X, in also killing the Dragon, Terrible and Traditional Enemy of the Kingdom of Point X. Thus Peace will Reign on Our people for Ever. Article 3. The Quest will be open to any man, of whatever origin or condition. Before departure however all contestants will register at Our Royal Ministry for Sport and War, where a special Office of Registration will be set up for the Issuing of Exit Visas. Article 4. Good luck to one and all, especially to one. Signed Carolus Magnus, Rex Puncti X. End of Proclamation.

In those days there will dwell in the forest a paper-cutter with his three sons, Nat the Nightman, Dan the Man of Dawn, and Perry Hupsos, who will all three dream of leaving their old father the paper-cutter and the mere raw material of sensation for the airy end-product. They will hear the Royal Herald's Proclamation on their small transistor and they will say to each other why not try our luck?

By right of birth I shall be the first to go will say Dan the Man of Dawn.

No will say Nat the Nightman, by tradition the youngest will inevitably win so I might as well spare you your defeats and probable deaths.

And Perry Hupsos will say let's take the middle way and leave all together. One will make straight for the mountain and have a very stiff climb, another will go round it westwards and the third will go round it eastwards, which should be longer but easier. One of us will surely succeed.

Then they will quarrel about who would take which road.

Perry Hupsos will say let's make it a combined operation. It won't matter which road because we'll keep each other informed of snares and progress by walkietalkie. Whoever should come first upon the dragon's lair will call the others and guide them and wait, studying the terrain. We shall plan the attack together and win together. We'll make a pact and sign it in our brotherly blood.

Then which one will have the princess and the kingdom? Dan the Man of Dawn will ask.

The one who will first find the dragon's lair will have the kingdom. The one who will find the fatal soft spot in the underbelly and shoot his arrow into it will have the princess. The third, whatever he may do to help, will get the treasure and become the richest man in the land.

Pooh, dreamer, that'll be bad economics and worse politics, what will be the value of a princess without a kingdom and a kingdom without a treasure? Besides, I shall not use an arrow but a sword.

And I shall use my atomic gun.

Meanwhile young Roland Fitzjohn, son of Lady Damaris Fitzjohn and John Briggs, Bank Director, will register and set out. So will Chuck Cherryblue and Mustapha and Nelson Nwankwo and many others, even Olivier Gómez de la Sierra, although a little old at thirty-five, and Jean-Luc de Rommède, who'll be thirty-two and a little tired of his second wife Chantal Berger.

Mysteriously all the contestants in the quest, whatever their ways and means, will meet the same witch, who could be called Beatrice de Umfraville why not. She will not be at all ugly, nor breathlessly beautiful but an ordinary citizen sitting at each one of the lower gates and selling painted flowers. Buy me a flower for luck, love, buy me a flower for luck.

Why hello aunt Bea will say Jean-Luc de Rommède what could possibly bring you here?

Ask no foolish questions and you'll be told no foolish lies, just buy me a flower and he will. So will quite a few others. Any contestant not buying a painted flower from Beatrice de Umfraville at any one of the city gates will very likely get no further in his quest.

For mysteriously all the contestants in the quest, whatever their ways and dubious ends, will meet the first donor on their way, who will be called Mark Woods, and he will ask them for their painted flower. The flowerless will be guided into the forest and get hopelessly lost, ending up as paper-cutters. Mark Woods will greet the successful candidates of this first ruthless elimination Hail Flower-bearer.

Oh hello great-uncle Mark will say Roland Fitzjohn could you be the first donor?

I shall done nothing unless you can pollinate the forest with your painted flower.

Well old man you must think that a poser, but I shall use the beehive on my coat of arms the motto of which as you should know will always be Keep Busy with a queen bee couchante and a swarm rampant.

Good, good, that'll do, waste no time my boy, just leave your coat of arms on this tall folio it'll do the trick and be on your way.

Oh hello cousin will drop from Olivier Gómez de la Sierra who will have the same idea running in his blood, as will Chuck Cherryblue but by marriage only and much more slowly as he won't be tothemannerborn, although his rhythm once found will be much faster. Mustapha without these social advantages will fail to mark the wood. Perry Hupsos will hit on the sublime notion of making the words bees and buzz do the work, then he will walk away and loyally inform his brothers by walkietalkie. Nelson Nwankwo will bring out his statistical ays and bees from his pocket computer in his head and the greetings will be declared closed.

The second donor will be Serge Dupont. Why hi dad will say Olivier could you be the second donor?

I shall done nothing son unless you can take this bridge

without coming to it.

Well, let me see. If it is built on the seven pillars of wisdom it should be easy for wisdom will never stand up against burning temptation.

That can't be the answer Serge Dupont will reply but the bridge will fall. You shouldn't get out of it so lightly he will say rather chagrined but go your way, there will be a third test, not to mention the dragon himself and you'll be bound to fail somewhere.

Roland and Jean-Luc will make similar pirouettes with pillars of cloud and of Hercules by Jove that could well be the answer will exclaim their cousin. Chuck will make the pillars tremble and fall with the sheer thumping of his battery on tape. Nelson will by computer analysis prove the pillars to be both inclusively and exclusively disjuncted and therefore non-existent in the system. And Perry? Perry will raise the whole bridge to a transcendental. Shall I inform my brothers? It wouldn't be any use, they wouldn't be able to do it. So he will walk on unwalkietalking and the secession will be declared closed.

The third donor will be Erik Lagerkvist. Why uncle Erik, Chuck will exclaim fancy meeting you and what can you do for me?

I shall do nothing nephewinlaw unless you can lag the quest with laurel sprig.

Sprig it with laurel? Why, I'll dialaureate you down you monologgerhead of quest.

Such vulgarity should not enter into the family, but I'll have to let you pass if only for kinship-in-Danelaw. The punkinship will not be good enough for Roland or Olivier or even Jean-Luc. It will be non-existent for Nelson Nwankwo. Perry Hupsos will try the transcendental trick again but fail, for crowns of laurel sprigs will always resist the transcendental.

There will however be two late starters, one to be called Mussa and the other Anon, a poor streetsweeper. The donors will have shut up shop too soon, so that Mussa and Anon will walk together through the woods and up the mountain, Mussa singing the wiles away and Anon sweeping the undergrowth. They will sweep and sing across the bridge, coming to it a long time after taking it as a craggy boulder that will join two high ledges over a deep gorge. And there on the other side will be the dragon's lair.

And there too they will find Chuck Cherryblue in full blast with his cassette, trying to rock the dragon into battle and the terrified princess into rock. But the Princess Fatima my Folly will still be wrapped in tail and the dragon won't battle. He will cover his ears with his insulating persienne wings and drown the noise in supersonic snores. Beyond him and still wrapped in tail, the Princess Fatima my Folly will lie in a dead faint.

Then Mussa will sing, of copper moons and ivory tusks and tame gazelles. At first nothing of his words or gentle pitch will pierce the battery of snores and loud jazz rock. But slowly, subsonically the dragon will absorb the enchantment through his iranian wings which will quiver and fall back. An emerald-encrusted eyelid will lift, then droop. Chuck's cassette will run out. He'll swiftly understand and panicking will change the cassette to a more gooey orchestration with lush violins. The poetry contest will last for days and nights innumerable or three, each poet closely watching for the dragon to turn round in ecstasy and reveal his fatal soft spot. But the dragon will be too well educated in legend, his pleasure will be but mim-ecstasy. During a cassette change he will suddenly breathe out fire and burn both poets to ashes. Poetic licence thus will be punished by poetic justice.

Then Anon the streetsweeper will walk down from his hiding place above the fray and start sweeping the dragon's tail around the princess's waist, gently talking to her meanwhile and reviving her. The dragon's tail will twitch and then relax, the streetsweeper will seize the princess by the hand, extract her from the tailclutch and move her back with gestures, all the while continuing to sweep the dragon's tail very slowly, softly, further and further up towards the lower body. Jewels will fall off, diamonds, emeralds, rubies, amethysts and sapphires and aquamarines, and bars of gold, silver, copper, uranium, platinum, magnesium, cobalt, palladium and many other precious metals long encrusted on the blackgold sweat, all of which the sweeper will clean away. The dragon's tail thus released will breathe more freely and shudder at the caresses. Up and up, over the dragon's arched back, for days and nights innumerable or three, the dragon will purr.

Don't be afraid my friend, I shall not burn you alive I'll give you my dragon's word. I shall always be grateful to you, why I might have died of multiple sclerosis. Finish your job, if you would be so kind, that I may be free of all this pore-clogging detritus, and you shall take the Princess Fatima my Folly back to her old father King Carolus Magnus of the Flowery Beard.

Some of it may hurt dear dragon, the ingots will be especially hard to get rid of.

Not at all, not at all, even your hard scrubbing will be as caresses to me. I shall be patient if you will be.

Slowly the sweeper Anon will work away, freeing the dragon of his atropheys. Trustfully the dragon will turn on his back. Anon will see the bare soft spot and will not touch it. The dragon will be his friend for ever.

I shall be your friend for ever Anon.

But dragon if I leave all this detritus here you will simply get encrusted again by lying on it for centuries. Shall I sweep it all up into the cave and block the cave?

That would be too much to ask, dear friend, you will be very tired. But you may call me Thuban.

Okay then. But unless you predefer to stifle in the golden treasury of civilization you could help me with your powerful tail, Thuban, and if any should get reencrusted into it I'll sweep the tail again.

Why gladly but you'd better get out of the way first.

So all the treasure will be buried except for scattered bits unreachable by the big tail.

I'll sweep those in with the broom.

No my friend, pick them up and take them with you, at least as much as you'll be able to carry in the princess's cloak, and sweep the rest in if you would be so kind.

And now farewell. I shall be your friend forever and the friend of your people and the friend of your descendants. If you should ever need me for some big job like dragondozing or some wise advice you will know where to find me, but in secret please. Tell that secret to no one, nor my name, and hand it on at your death only to one man, that you'll choose for his humility, not to any politician for instance, not even among your own close descendants. Otherwise all the trouble will start again. Will you promise?

I shall not hand it on at all, Thuban, nor will the princess.

Not at all will say the princess speaking for the first time.

Indeed that would be the wisest course, in view of the chain reaction of rumour and information. You will be wiser than the kingdom could hope and the secret will die with you. But you will both live long, under my protection, and thus leave a powerfully blessed memory of your reign which may with luck influence future generations for a while. And now goodbye. Come, he will falter with a balloon of a pearly tear in his huge left eye, come and see me now and again, I shall miss you. And the princess. And your broom.

We will, we will, on every anniversary of our friendship. Secretly.

Good, good. Well now off with you and he will turn brusquely towards the edge of the ledge and plunge down the gorge into the river far below to soothe his itchy scales. The river will hiss and smoke.

Where will he live, sweeper? the princess will ask speaking for the second time.

Oh he'll find another lair.

I shall love you always she'll say, speaking for the third time.

And so they will return and marry and live unhappily ever after and have many children, owing a terrible allegiance and yearly tribute of virgins and other precious stones in mounting interest and inflation to the faithless and flailing return of the repressed prodigy.

Out of the eyes thighs arms cheeks flanks shins of men women and children the guinea-worm will crawl the angry voice of my lover substitute will say close to my ear so as not to wake anyone. To prevent proliferation they will not cut it but merely coil and fix it on a twig until the whole of it comes out. And if I should bring them clean cloth and beg them to filter the black water they'll say white man keep your fetish it won't work on the worm-god our fetish to whom we must sacrifice more birds or he'll become even angrier. What would you have us do? The speaker will be called Father Mark Woods.

But Father why should it be you alone, couldn't the State do something, and what about their own European-trained doctors?

My dear they wouldn't go out there, not into the bush, and as for the State it couldn't care less. The president will go on ordering his people to shake their bottoms in his praise and to sing songs about how their country will do without the white men and return to its native culture, they will fare him well in songs and bottoms next time he'll leave in his Mercedes and private plane and London suit and American sunglasses to have some over-eating ailment treated in a Swiss clinic. They won't even see the contradiction. The white men will continue to be hated as neo-colonist and venerated as sacred milch-cow-towing to the very traditions that will continue to pre-fabricate underdevelopment already in the swaddled limbs and fingers of their infants on their mothers' backs.

But what about the international welfare organizations and the Nwankwo project?

They won't succeed, he should go back and live there before

94

uttering such tired generalizations. Look rather at the guinea-worms, they'd express more of the thirdworld sickness than all the statistics of international welfare orgies or intrigues to buy up dictators and prop them up till they fall down.

I should like to buy myself a dictator who will be venerhated as a sacred milchcowtow and who'll say listen we promise, but first, a station break, telling us to slim to eat cookies to save to spend to live it up to live it down to vote rightleft of centre protest obey love one another shoot one another with toy deathrays for little boys and little girls holding the instruments for little boys to make a toy robot from a readymade kit no real thinking requirements. Stay with us, don't go away go solar and stop trying to be Atlas it'll never be a woman's job. Will anyone visit you?

No, only the postman around eleven if he should have anything for me, and possibly the farmer, but normally he'd only be around with his tractor in that maizefield behind the house, fairly soon by the look of it, but he wouldn't hear or see anything.

Yeah and until he gets around to it we won't see anyone coming into the lane from the road. Okay we'll keep her in the attic, she must never come down even to pee we'll have to go on emptying her slops.

Well, that won't be hard, they'll only be nice clean compound interests I'll put them on the compost heap.

How soon will she be indoctrinated?

It'll take a while still, she'll go on having ideological setbacks with vomiting and diarrhoea but slowly she'll get hooked I guess.

Not too slowly, we shouldn't stay here too long.

No you shouldn't.

Oh stop thinking about yourself and your personal comfort Mira, be hospitable and open-minded, less mean in fact.

Well I'll be damned, after —

Shut up, just try and increase the dose real fast.

I would seem to be unpopular with these characters. How long shall I continue to rush into overfriendliness obscurely to

95

make up for the overfreeness of my solitude? Soon the Thuban cycle should emerge from the cloudy skies, in advance of Orion and Cygnus and Cassiopeia behind which Andromeda will return as me. When Mr Knight the postman comes I shall go out to meet him, as if to save him getting out of his scarlet van, as if all were normal and instead of digging up thistles or feeding pigs I were simply working inside, painting the kitchen fixing the electricity reading Herodotus. Perhaps Orion will send me another emotionally blocked postcard with a star drawn from his belt.

No of course, Hans won't trust me, he'll go out himself to meet the postman, who will merely suppose him a new lover, and jealous of my mail. Roberto'll be back this afternoon Mira but don't tell him at once about our feeding lark, he'll be bringing quite a bit of bread from Sean and I'll have to think things out first okay?

Kay boss.

But after all, why shouldn't I get letters?

Dear Mira,

Please forgive me for writing to you without an intro-duction as it were, but at my very old age I might perhaps be permitted to break a few small social rules.

How should I know of your existence or have your address? Not from my nephew Orion, you may be surprised to learn, but from your uncle Kurt, an old friend of mine, on a visit. Also you will no doubt at least know of me through Orion.

I hope you will be lenient if I express my deep unease about him, and more especially about his relation to you. Are you so sure that you really understand him? After his experiences, he would be bound to have a certain block-age, to need unusual depth of foresight, but one which should not show itself as foreknowledge, as a tendency to enclose and finalize him within one image you may have of him. For even though he may in fact never evolve out of his blockage, it should not be anyone else's role to decide that he will not, and either to enclose him in that or else to opt out, feeling all the while that you will be inventing him. There should be a more creative middle way, which would be as it were to fulfil your responsibility up to a certain demarcation line but not beyond it.

Of course this may well be too late and if so please be indulgent towards an old lady's meddling, which may strike you as coming from another world but which will I hope be kindly taken as kindly meant. With best regards,

Yours sincerely,

Lizvieta Grant.

Dear Ms Inkytea, the other letter will start with innocuous hopes of wellbeing at reception and that my silence won't be due to illness or some other contre-temps, to be followed by five pages of electronic typewriter on the brainwashing of woman from birth into thinking marriage the only desirable thing in life and themselves as having something distinctly wrong with them should they fail to get some man to the altar and more of same on the collusion of religions philosophies and psychiatries in the tailormaking of societies to male needs, all out of some antique pamphlet, which I'll skip to find out what in fact she'll be wanting this time, ah, here. However, since all these evils will no longer ever cause her any unhappiness for she'll thank her lucky stars no man will ever manage to drag her to skip on. While there will never be any ready-made cure for human grief and sorrow as such, no doubt the misery of such women will greatly be eased in a world where everyone will have ceased to think there could be anything whatever wrong, either psychologically or socially, with a woman 'living alone' or not having 'a man in her life', whether this be by accident or by choice.

What on earth will she be getting at now? Clearly 'Emma' (as a friend of hers, who shall be nameless, will call all those women hellbent on educating another), ah, so that'll be it, her old kick, and her 'pupil' will soon be on the way out, both victims of that brainwashing drug, albeit in different ways. Emmas will always be childless (and may be grieving over that fact) or, more often than not, a married gal with a load of probs though she'd rather die than admit it, this as an effect of the drug; or she'll be a married but discarded gal, like you. As for the pupil, she'll nearly always be one of those creatures who may be beginning to think that there might indeed be a thing or two wrong with her for not having made it to the altar, which would be why she'd listen to Emma in the first place.

Considering that I would never, never analyse or criticize *you*, or tell you how to live and manage your relationships, it would be about time, surely, that you returned the compliment. Besides, how the hell could anybody, whoever they might be, so much as begin to sympathize with or wish to help over the problems of anyone else if they're going to be relentlessly told what's wrong with them before they can so much as open their mouths in that endeavour, or worse, have to submit to your grinning like a blood Cheshire cat at every damn remark I might make about anything at all? So how about packing it in and having a bash at normal behaviour eh?

However, if you can't or won't return that compliment then it'll all be bloody hopeless. As for the tragic aspect of the matter I shall refuse to shed any more tears upon it. Indeed I shall soon cease to think of you in terms of someone who should be teaching me the glories of literary criticism and philosophy but just as an Emma, something no woman will ever want again, much less need in her life, and which future generations may well regard as just one of those things that went with the drug.

But every story will have as you should know at least two sides and you should not content yourself with but one third of the picture, or else you'll be making a big mistake you mark my words. You cannot play both your beau role as cultural instructor and your role as tragedy queen for ever having her peace shattered so snap out of it, or else find yourself another sidekick, and much joy may it give you.

I trust there will be no need for further communication from you, indeed, any letter you may write will go straight to the w.p.b. unread.

Yours sincerely,

Ethel Thuban.

The third letter will be an acknowledgement of an application for a job, accompanied by regrets that the humanities ancient or modern would not be taught any further in that university owing to the drastic cuts in teaching posts and radical alteration of programmes or vice versa perhaps. The last will be from my other sidekick sado-escaperoute Willy, who'll blessedly be on a lecture-tour about programme-cuts, pseudo-counting the days to our tender reunion. Let me add, however, that if Hyperboreans exist beyond the north wind, there must also be Hypernotians beyond the south hey what d'yer think yer doing?

Surely Hans you'll have to allow me to read my mail?

Yes but you'll have to allow me to censor it.

Please yourself, you won't find it very interesting, a lot of bourgeois tizzies you'd call them and besides, how could anyone outside know of my predicament with you since you won't allow me to write?

Stop asking questions will you and let me read, and you'd better learn to bend to our discipline, go upstairs and relieve Gisela.

I'll have to feed the pigs first.

Obey me will you.

Pigs first, underprivileged.

If that's not a bourgeois tizzy what is? Don't you know anything about agronomics, do you really suppose your back-to-the-soil escapism will contribute one particle to the new society? Do you —

I could feed at least one pig during one speech.

Okay okay have it your way but get on with it. Women!

It would seem, however, that I shall have to alter the tree

99

and tag myself on to it as niece of Kurt Krank, which would also explain my link to Hans as cousin, just as aunt Lizvieta's letter would explain the link with the shadow-mind Orion. Perhaps I should press the LIST key to re-vision the whole regrafted tree and have the whole thing clearer in my telematic head:

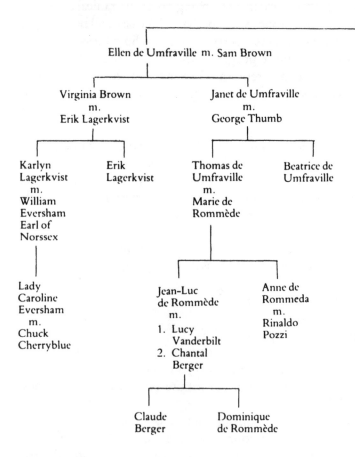

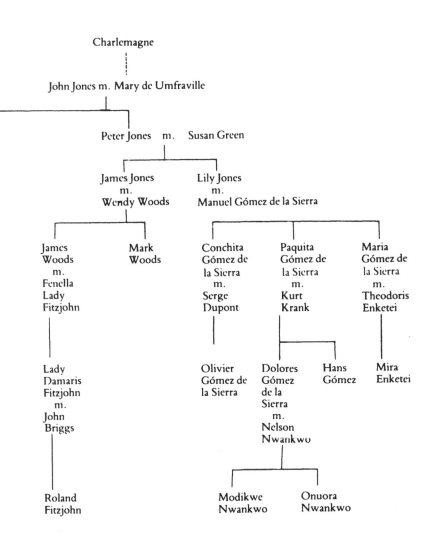

Charlemagne

John Jones m. Mary de Umfraville

Peter Jones m. Susan Green

James Jones   Lily Jones
m.   m.
Wendy Woods   Manuel Gómez de la Sierra

James   Mark   Conchita   Paquita   Maria
Woods   Woods   Gómez de   Gómez de   Gómez de
m.   la Sierra   la Sierra   la Sierra
Fenella   m.   m.   m.
Lady   Serge   Kurt   Theodoris
Fitzjohn   Dupont   Krank   Enketei

Lady   Olivier   Dolores   Hans   Mira
Damaris   Gómez de   Gómez   Gómez   Enketei
Fitzjohn   la Sierra   de la
m.   Sierra
John   m.
Briggs   Nelson
                                      Nwankwo

Roland   Modikwe   Onuora
Fitzjohn   Nwankwo   Nwankwo

If these characters are thus going to link me to themselves and to each other, the one reproaching me for not fulfilling my responsibilities and for overfulfilling my role, the other for playing contrary roles they would probably be dead right, or even dead perhaps, part of my low parametabolic threshold which would enclose deaf demolishers within one image that will never be but one third of the picture. They don't seem to like me much anyway.

Perhaps I should find myself another sidekick function such as getting apprized of certain facts which may come as a shock to me, if only they would, and so relax and sit comfortably in the bowroll of tragedy monarchperson which I cannot have as well as that of culture-vulture of at any rate myself prometheanbound to an electronic lover substitute, alone among pigs and men.

And since even a polygonal story should have at least two sides in all intergnashional farewell orgies, how about packing it in and having a bash at normal behaviour eh, so as to get bashed again as whipping boy despite my morseled-out attempts to break free or go shiating on, turning the other cheek to sheer cheek as sitting target for the unclear missiles of affreux dizzy acts or as wailing wall of blame beyond the demarcation line or bowstring frontier that will boomerang back and much joy may it give me.

The volcano may erupt any time during this legislation or the next, the more urgent the predictions the slower the reactions of the Council European or World in the rush with which we shall speed through history. Better find myself another sidekick such as the warrior's rest in nomansland, or better still be relaxed and comfortably seated inside some other walloping leviathan and curl up with a book of genetic information so as to avoid the danger of gender, to be nevertheless bashed for lying incestuously with oh my prophetic soul my uncle Gigo, forecaster of his own poleaxe who'll have dunnit all, vocally equivocal in the slow gas-chambers of sibylisation.

I Claudius Caesar should clearly replace Charlemagne of the

flowery beard despite the lack of offspring that will only be
due to the death of all characters on stage except Horatio and
more things in heaven and earth and of course Fortinbras and
his army.
The fault dear Brutus won't be in our stars but in

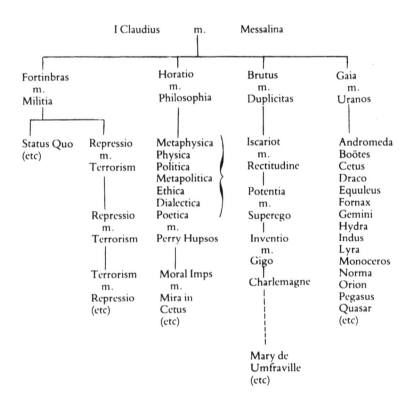

Hello, what can Mr Jolly be wanting I'll say suddenly, gazing from the kitchen window.

Who?

The farmer, he's going to come here, across the cow-pasture.

Bugger him, rush up and warn Gisela to be extra quiet, if necessary to inject the prisoner, then come back, we'll talk to him together, you'll introduce me as your cousin John or something, I'll think up a few peasantries to say.

Right.

Okay now relax, Hans, he'll only be coming to scythe my bit of field in exchange for the grass, and maybe help me with Minny Ha-ha's litter and I won't be able to choose another day, not in harvest time, so he'll be around all afternoon.

Oh shit, and Roberto'll be coming in with the bread.

Keep your cool Hans and let me handle it for once, do you think me friendless and without visitors, he won't think twice about your presence. And talking of harvest may I remind you that my small daughter will soon be coming back from her grandparents in Greece so you'll have to move on to Point Y or wherever now smile.

May I introduce Dr and Mrs Nelson Nwankwo, of WHO, Mr Erik Lagerkvist, of UNICEF.

Mes hommages, madame, glad to know you doctor.

Don't you remember me then Mr Lagerkvist?

Er

Of course we would all look alike to you.

Oh take that chip down Nelson, don't you sometimes confuse faces and names in multinational gatherings? I would.

Surely you would not, madame, or at least, you would never be at a loss.

Well, I don't know. If you'll excuse me for speaking of myself for one moment and my radio-programme, a sort of problem programme for lonely people and insomniacs, I shall for ever dread that night when some Jenny or Jimmy will call again to tell me their sequel and I shan't remember. Of course the filter-cabin will always help but still.

104

It must indeed be quite nerve-racking madame, even with your great presence of mind, especially with no faces even, only voices. I should have no such excuse doctor but let me see, wouldn't you be, yes of course, Cassandra! Now come, you mustn't mind a little legpull my dear friend, for indeed I shall make up for everything by congratulating you most sincerely on your excellent report. It will open many avenues let me assure you, and will suggest many ways and means.

Providing it first open the many eyes closed to the avenues of ways and means.

Oh believe me doctor the eyes will never be as closed as you may think, glory be to Argus. Keep hammering away at it my friend, do not despair, above all do not despair, as your most charming wife will not, excuse-me?

My only wife sir.

Ha, you will have your little joke. I shall stand corrected, your very charming wife will not, in her fine task, her very fine role, we must each do our bit for the misery of mankind must we not? And now will you kindly excuse me, I must have a word with my ambassador. Will you both do me the honour of dining at my house quite soon? Mes hommages, madame, doctor goodnight, à bientôt.

Quel con!

Shsh, he'll hear you darling.

Not in this international cacophony.

Shall we slip away? I must tuck the children in and rest a bit before going to prepare my programme.

Well, I ought to stick around a bit longer if you don't mind, but you could slip away.

No, all right I'll stay, but not too long please oh good evening.

I hope it won't be too long let me see, 5,000,000,000,000 at 18% compound after three years 8,215,160,000 after seven years 15,927,369,500,000, well, interest could degress half a percent per year then it would be 14,559,265,950,000 I'll have to stick to these small sums till help comes although I could take vaster risks within the mind construct of high finance and the perpetual excitement of the movement of capital. They'll never understand that they can't win, the dolts, trying to attack Leviathan with a bow and arrow, let them think they'll be doping me with Marxism I'll be able to hold out, it'd take a product 5,000% more powerful than that to indoctrinate me as long as I continue to calculate myself into existence out of imaginary sums, increasing myself per day per minute if necessary, after all every financial operation might be pure fiction from my point of view. Let's try 50 billion at 19% over ten years, oh Mammon, another anti-capitalist meal, if only they'd let me listen to the gnome instead or the Stock Exchange.

Splendid Roberto, but leave it in the false bottom for the moment eh, come in and have a rest then I'll have things to tell you.

But won't she be starving? Forgive me for taking so long boss but guess what, it'll be more than you'll expect and not from Sean at all but Carlo. Carlo Magno bless him he'll always turn up trumps.

Fine, fine, now put the car away and padlock the barn, but keep the key readily available in case we have to make a quick getaway.

But —

Get on with it, I'll be needing you later for radio-monitoring, we'll be short-handed what with cooking cleaning shopping and guarding the prisoner in turns, and we'll have a planning conference soon. Now put it away.

But mother why, why would you want to send me away like that to some unknown uncle in Paris, why should he want me there anyway?

Your cousin, not a direct uncle, your cousin Olivier, son of a cousin of my father's, would like you to visit him, Roland, stop fussing. And you must do something, you won't go to university, or into the army, or into the Foreign Office, or even to the City where your father could give you an entry and a leg-up, so you might as well perfect your French and open your mind while you make it up, your mind of course, not your French. He may give you advice, or ideas, he may suggest an opening over there, in real estate for instance.

You want me to become a real estate agent? Jesus, real or unreal I'll never be an agent for anyone. I wanna be on my own, free to move around.

Well, I could try the Earl of Norssex, a vague relation, he might help, or his brother-in-law, a Swede and a big shot at the United Nations or something. Or I could send you to Italy, to a distant cousin, the Franco-Italian branch, but it might be more awkward to recontact her besides, Italy these days —

Why all this bloody relation lark, why should I have anything in common with cousin Olivier or cousin Whatever merely because of a crummy genealogical tree? I'd rather be a mongrel and piss on your silly tree.

Now don't be vulgar darling and don't lose your temper. And it needn't be real estate, it could be insurance or business or even publishing or anything, but your father will only support you till the equivalent of the end of your studies, and if you won't study you'll have to find some other way of earning your living. You should be grateful that he'll do all that, most young people —

Grateful, always grateful. I'll be grateful if he'll just leave me alone, I'll grow up without his damn support, I'll hitch round the world and work my way if necessary, I'll go to Katmandu to Kampala to Kyoto to Kuala Lumpur to Kinshasa to —

Won't that be a bit zigzaggy?

You shouldn't do that Mira.

Do what, Hans?

Link everyone like that, we'd call it damn Gründlichkeit on my side of the family. You won't see the wood for the sodding genealogy. You'll have to learn that trees will need pruning every year, some branches will have to be sacrificed for others to grow strong, just like evolution.

And revillusion?

And revolution if you like. Now if you want to link everyone up at all cost why don't you dial Dolores?

What!

After the Perry Hupsos Show. My big sister, your cousin, Our Lady of Dolors. We'll give her a message on the air, live, and see how she keeps her cool. I won't, she'd recognize my voice.

You crazy Hans? They'd trace the call.

No, it'll be very brief, and you'll tell the filter-cabin some poppycockcrow.

But they'd take the number and talk to me first, to avoid repetition of woes, or in case of trouble, of sex-maniac insults, or even in case they lose you, so that they can ring back, and callers will always be kept waiting for ages on phone-ins.

Oh. Well, maybe. Well, we'll give up on that one. Pity, I'd sure like to hear how she'd keep her sympathetic cool. Now, to work. First, timetables, and talking of time, what would all this be about a kid coming home? Could you have given birth to get rid of us or out of pique or something?

Why should I tell you? But I could do anything with you lot.

Well cut it out.

But in any case Hans, after the summer I'll be going into town for lectures, and to see my supervisor, Professor Swann, and maybe to try for jobs again, I won't be cut off here all the time I'll have other work to do.

Lectures? Supervisor? Supervising what?

My thesis, I'll be going back to it, on dolepay I'll have time on my hands now, especially in winter. On the philosophy of history.

Philosophy? History? Pah. In the next civilization there won't be any history, let alone any philosophy of it.

You'll abolish it then, like freedom? Killing the goose that'll lay the golden ages? You'll need a wide margin of terror for that.

Cut the wisecracks. We simply won't care about it, we'll devalue it, so it will disappear.

How?

We won't rehandle or reinterpret it, we'll create history and forget about it, events will be our instant history, but history as events not history as discourse. We won't allow you verbiage-mongers to add the water, we'll scatter the self-consuming ashes to the winds and move on into the next instant. That'll be one thing less for kids to break their brains on and be made miserable with in competition, and there'll be others, plenty of other things we'll drop in the next civilization mark my words.

I will, full marks. But meanwhile you'll have to move on to Point Y. Should I assume that Point Z will be the end of this civilization?

You could be right baby, you could be right.

That'll be charming.

Look, dope, I'll do the violence, you'll do the deploring but later, okay? Meanwhile you'lluv played a great little role yourself in the whole operation.

So that I'd be one of the first people you'll eliminate of course. Like kicking away the Platonic ladder.

Platonic my foot.

Precisely.

Now shut up will you, we gotta work. Roberto come down, Gisela'll relieve you then we'll give her the works.

When in nomansland do as nomans will.

The problem for the minister of technology will be to ensure that Britain should master the exploitation of foreign information systems in such a way as to avoid what might be called the flight of questions, as it were, abroad, and to favour the preparation of specialized scientific technology information of a quality recognized by the international scientific community, so as to dispose of an exchange currency and organize distribution circuits in such a way that the general network of utilisers should be perpetually irrigated. Thus we must give priority to the national independence of data banks in all technological areas of knowledge, technico-economic and technico-juridical, and create a centralized service. Independence will be crucial if we do not want questions to be addressed elsewhere.

Thus uncle Ego the commanding general will feed his and the enemy's order of battle into the digital disputer and feed in the question should I advance or retreat and the disputer will flash his reply yes, yes what, yes SIR, oh uncle Ego how could you?

Why shouldn't I? Leave my political ideas alone Jean-Luc, how would you like it if I said how could you to your smart business deals and your smart marriages and smart adventures on the side? Just let me be and let me and Rinaldo live by our beliefs. Stop trying to sweep the carpet from under my feet it won't wash.

It might dry clean.

Oh really —

And what sort of carpet is it if I can sweep it away so easily? What would you want me to say after all, little sister?

Oh nothing, nothing after all that you wouldn't be programmed to say by your environmental ideology.

And you'd be an exception to that rule?

Yes I would and why not, thanks to dialectical thinking, and I wish people wouldn't go on at me all the time with preconceptions and without bothering even to read my books. If you did you might begin to see sense and realize that this smart

110

world of yours won't last much longer and to do something about it. For even if your way of life were only an adjustment, a using of the system to survive it, wouldn't that be simply conscience-salving, an interiorization of a deep unease? Personally I don't see the need to interiorize my own adjustments to that extent.

No, they would seem rather evident. Look, call it what you will Anne darling but let's have a whisky and relax before Rinaldo comes home, he mustn't find us in a kids' squabble must he? Talking of which I'll be seeing aunt Bea next week, I'll be going to London on business and will try and pop down there for a day. What shall I tell her from you?

Give her my love.

Anything else?

Well, general news of me, and my last book, oh, that won't interest her, well, anything you like, tell her I'll be writing soon.

Okay. Erm. Tell me about Rinaldo, will he get this promotion? Thanks. Let's drink to that. Won't it place him in danger though, from terrorists?

Heavens no.

Oh?

Oh don't be absurd Jean-Luc, he simply won't be high-placed enough, it wouldn't be worth their while. Anyway he should get it, the promotion, not the danger.

Okay okay. Tell me, don't you ever fall in love? I couldn't live without falling in love. Often.

Well, if I did, and there'd be plenty of opportunities, I wouldn't be happy. I'd probably —

Load the poor man with your uneasy conscience in disguideology?

Now stop it big brother I warn you, how do you think I can relax if you keep on at me? What's the matter with everyone?

Everyone?

Oh all right, if you want me to confess to an unhappy love affair to ease *your* conscience I'll confess, but not now, Rinaldo'll be home any minute. Tomorrow. If I still feel like it mind. You may have a way of twisting me round your elder fraternal finger and making me feel I'd like to get this or that off my chest but it probably won't last the night. Rinaldo will come in soon and change the atmosphere and restore my peace of mind and sense of loyalty and —

Hush little sister, you'll do exactly as you please, if you want a shoulder I'll be one if not not, I'll forget about it okay? And forgive me for needling you.

Forgive, yes, but don't keep taking the mere utterance of that word as licence to go on and pursue your advantage for ever.

What advantage? If I have to pursue it I don't have it. I'll pursue you if you're not careful and plunge you into incestual torments and then where will your clear and super-adjusted moral imperatives be?

Unless Rinaldo comes in soon to change the atmostfearic density around the nebulae the exploding novae the white dwarves blue giants moral imps and gnomic misguideologies on all sides, indeed the red giant of Trier might turn into a grey gnome of Zurich, streetsweepers into kings, geniuses into plastic bottles, citadels into sitting targets for unclear missiles and smiles into similes of cheshirecat grins and vice versa, our crowing achievement to go round the world on an inferior monologue, bowroller-skating along to prevent the flight of questions elsewhere or to pursue the advantages we'll have already lost for ever.

Take a shape, any shape, and draw it on a piece of paper my lover substitute will say, reproduce it on another, altering just one parameter, a vertical line for instance, to an infinitesimal degree, and then another degree and another, and continue thus for every possible parameter. The thousands of sheets of paper, the millions of minutes and energy molecules you will spend to select the few aesthetically satisfying results according to mysterious principles as yet unknown and based on the mood of the moment, on cultural models and other imponderables, could be saved by putting the whole process through the prestidigital computer, which will retain in its phenomenal memory every single shape, the final selection through imponderables being then much fresher from lack of exhaustion. Switch it off I must feed the pigs well I'll take it with me to the President of France who will be driving his auto-satisfaction down to Rambouillet for a working weekend with the King of the Medes.

I shall in fact be unpresentable, unheaded and dishevelled, smelling of pigs, unpersoned, and my secret lover will speak to me in secret electronics only, over the ionosphere, or hide me away behind the battlements or send me to my ivory loftware should he have royal guests such as Amalgamemnon. Unless he exhibit the hidden sibyl in him and read their hands their handwriting their dreams their entrails to keep the dialogue going.

There will be computers for self-fulfilling prophecies for what will prophecy be but instant history diluted with tiered generalizations and a margin of terror, add half a databank of crowing achievement and six face-saving devices finely chopped. As for election results they will be divulged in less than no time by galloping vote projections so that the speedier the media the slower but surer will be the disenfranchising by disenchantment what, nine months of crap for three minutes of suspense? And what if the third millenium after the third-world war refuse this confuturism, what if it predefer that the great deeds of men should after all be forgotten, whether Greeks or foreigners and, especially, the causes of the wars between them? For since the father of fibstory will be relegated with all his descendants to the planet's garbage-satellite and pollute the ionosphere we'll only have the world as bookend to look to.

But I too shall join the guerillas. Why should I marry Mustapha and dream for ever of my gentle poet, dead among African rocks with his dark eyes staring at the sun? I shall escape and cover my breasts under a soldier's tunic and learn to shoot like the crackiest of troops, and if they discover me I shall insist, or escape again to other battles in the north, hiding in the bottom of a boat and sailing up the sea to Egypt, or join

113

the Palestinians whose Allah will accept me as fighting daughter of a more southern Allah, I shall have to listen more carefully to the village radio and learn which tribes otherwise I'll never understand the places and names and peoples and causes I'll be fighting for. Because if I die and what else would there be I must die for something good. I want to fight the world but for the right people I must learn which and where and find them. I shall not stay here I'll steal clothes and provisions and escape and go north by the stars.

Now let me think, what shall I forget this time? Oh the cream. No? Not for you? Lizvieta will like some and I just might too. Yes, well may you admire my painted flowers, thank you Jean-Luc, you'll always be my favourite nephew, well my only nephew yes but if I had others they wouldn't be so adorably polite, they couldn't be could they? But the flies, they will settle on the drying paint and get stuck and spoil everything, the flies in the ointment you might say.

But how do you get the flowers so real aunt Bea? And then, so many, everywhere, on all the mirrors, the windows, glass doors, kitchen and bathroom surfaces, walls even, we could be in a magic garden, why and the china, surely you don't make your own pottery as well?

Why not dear boy why not? I must pottily potter about and occupy my elderly leisure, and I can't garden any more and can't afford a gardener like my dear friend Lizvieta, so what should I do with my old front lawn but pave it and shut it out and bring the garden inside? Yes dear take the tray. As for looking-glasses, well at my age I'd rather look at painted flowers. Of course I won't pretend to get the freshness and fragrance and sheer surprise and joy at the first peep and sudden blossming out.

No of course not Bea, but let me tell you something young man —

Jean-Luc, dear, my nephew, Mrs Lizvieta Grant, a neighbour.

Yes yes —

But of course, I'll lose my very memory next, still, better than my manners, cream Lizvieta?

Never offer cream with tea to a Russian, Bea, you should know that by now, and talking of bees I'll tell you this young man, the bees will buzz in all summer, big bees who should know better, mistaking them for real flowers. Just like Whatshisname and the grapes.

How extraordinary. Do you suppose they make painted honey?

Oh what a charming nephew, Lizvieta wouldn't you like to have such a charming nephew? Painted honey! I must remember that. But I'll surely forget, like everything else. And before I forget, tell me about Anne, my favourite niece. Forgive us Lizvieta if we talk family for one brief moment.

Go ahead, go ahead, let's hope he'll give you more news than my nephew, equally charming I'd like to assure you.

How can anyone be charming and not give news?

Now don't try and rival nephews with me Beatrice it won't succeed. Charm will always be a very individual thing, like love, mysterious and many-splendoured —

Please Lizvieta dear just let me get my ration of news will you? Have a biscuit meanwhile and keep quiet like a good girl. Now then dear boy tell me all, about your sister, yourself, your wife, your children, your father and mother in that order.

Gracious, I'll need a whole tin of biscuits.

Well you can always leave dear, and take away the bright

115

image of your curiosity satisfied. Take no notice Jean-Luc and start, ready steady go.

Dear aunt Bea, I don't know where to start.

At the beginning, in the prescribed order.

Well, Anne —

Could she be happy with this Potty fellow?

Pozzi. Rinaldo Pozzi. Of course, very happy. Very busy too, she'll have another book out in December.

Another book. No children?

No.

How odd, with an Italian. And none in view?

How should I know, aunt Bea?

Or rather you couldn't care less? Wouldn't you like to be an uncle?

Not particularly.

Why not, because you don't like being a father?

Now come, aunt Bea, don't invent, I'll give you news but don't pry into non-existent problems.

She'll paint problems too, very lifelike. No, no more biscuits thank you.

So Anne's going to be famous. Well well. What will her book be about? Will it be a good story at least?

That would depend on your point of view. It'll be as usual about politics, dialectics, the lessons of history.

Good heavens, as if we ever profited from those. Why dredge up the past I should have thought it couldn't teach us a thing in this rapidly changing world, and all we should bother with should be the present and the future. Especially the present, since out of it will come the future.

Why Bea, how well you would get on with my nephew, he'd say exactly the same.

Which would tend to show my dear that polite political banalities will remain much the same from generation to generation.

What on earth could be the matter with you Bea, the presence of your nephew shouldn't be an excuse to nag at mine all the time, why you don't even know him.

116

Because I don't invite myself to tea on the day of his one and only visit years later than he should come.

Well if that's the way it's going to be I'll leave.

Oh please Mrs Grant, please don't let my visit spoil your friendship and neighbourliness. Remember that I shall leave, your friendship will remain, and also that, well, the great charm of aunt Bea will always be her, well, eccentricity.

Could that be another name for plain rudeness? But you may well be right, Jean-Luc, if I may so call you.

Shall I introduce him to you a third time?

Jean-Luc, such a nice name, and indeed a very polite and charming young man let me congratulate you Bea.

Why me? Congratulate my brother, I'll transmit.

True, I won't then. And you must remember, Jean-Luc, that we Slavs will always be very susceptible people, with a tragic view of life and —

Translate: one mustn't pull her leg. What I shall miss most from having no garden will be the toad. 'Imaginary gardens with real toads in them'. If he should come to yours Lizvieta remember to stroke him lightly down the back, when he'll have got used to your presence of course, especially if you play music on summer nights. But never, never pull his leg.

Would he like Russian music?

German, French, Italian, English, Austrian, Spanish, American. But Russian, I would very much doubt it.

Then your analogy must fall flat on its face.

Most analogies will if you push them off balance. Just like tightrope walkers.

Or painted problems. Or prying into the future.

Or prying into other people's nephews.

By pure chance as you must surely know, and why invite, why press me to join you, if you don't enjoy showing him off?

Ladies, ladies, do you always go on like this? Or could you be showing off to me?

Now stop it all of you. Hypothesis one, we'll have to leave, corollary, we must a) decide between Point Y and Point Z, b) plan it very carefully, the risks will be tremendous. Hypothesis two, we'll stay right here till the end of August and even after the kid's arrival.

And Tess? In hypothesis two?

No problem. A kid around will make things look normal to the farmer, the postman, the pig-butcher and the rest of your rich social life here. It won't be for long anyway, we'll just have to forbid her the attic on grounds of privacy of guests, Gisela and I will sleep up there as nice uncle and aunt, Roberto'll use the campbed in the kitchen so that the kid can have her little room as usual and think nothing strange. We'd have to take up all the radio equipment though, and that'll be a nuisance, it might encourage the prisoner, even though she won't hear anything without earphones.

I'd prefer hypothesis one.

You would. Anything to preserve your bourgeois tranquillity.

Not only. For your own sakes it would be crazy to stay so long in the same place.

On the contrary, we must lie low till they slacken, till the journalists get tired of non-news and give their attention to other events, of which there'll be plenty when the season follows the silly season. Then, when we're forgotten, we'll move.

If I may finish. The danger wouldn't be the same place but this place. Anyone may get suspicious, the farmer or the meterman or even friends, for although you may think me friendless and alone you'd be quite wrong, anyone passing through the region on their return from holidays might take it into their heads to come and say hello, even expecting to be put up, friends, ex-students, ex-colleagues, ex-lovers, anyone, then you'd really be in a mess.

Crap, they'd see guests here already, surely your friends and lovers wouldn't be that rude, you'd give them tea or even a meal and they'd move off.

Unlike you, yet you'd hope they'd have the bourgeois virtues? And afterwards, how long would you stay, the farmer may think it strange that I should have permanent guests in this tumbledown farm, uninhabitable in winter I should warn you, except by me, a Spartan Trojan, living in the kitchen only and working in layers of woollies and overcoats.

We'll take that fridge when we come to it. All right, you'd prefer one, how about you Roberto?

I don't know Hans I —

You don't know you don't know? What does that mean, you should vote and therefore know.

First I should think shouldn't I? We should discuss. And you should lead, which, like governing, should mean to foresee.

And what do you suppose I'd be doing, right now?

Okay okay but you may foresee wrong. Why for instance would they slacken and forget, like an ordinary kidnapping? The whole government and financial world ought to be collapsing according to your supposed previsions, so how could they forget?

Precisely. If world economy collapses they'll have other things to think about. Now shut your trap and vote.

Well I can hardly do both.

Vote, slob.

Well if you're right it wouldn't matter whether we'd stay or move, but okay, let's stay.

Good. And Gisela'll say the same when she comes down, so you'll be outvoted Mira.

Naturally. No one will ever listen to me. Be it upon your own heads, and alas on mine as accomplice, albeit unwilling, and besides, beware of your prisoner.

Be it, alas, albeit, beware, what d'you think you are, an oracle, a voice in the wilderness?

Cassandra Castratrix O Cassiopeia, heavenly doubleyou so poised between Cepheus King of Ethiopia and his daughter Andromeda, circling the polestar which might be Cepheus himself by 5000 A.D. or even Thuban thousands of years later, I'll double you for quits for what will the future be but a past to be constantly deleted with new ways of achieving the anticipated which themselves will create shifts in the madlanes of memory so that nothing will be exactly as you shall one day

see it in retrospect, otherwise you would grow big with expectoration and explode, now or at the end of time the great
corrector and corrupter of meaning.

Take the dolphin for instance my lover substitute will say in
a pedantic voice, that will leap briefly into view just above the
horizon in May below the Swan, dissect it and analyse the
contents of its stomach and you will find many and various
traces of poisonous minerals, mercury and hydrocarbons and
other pollutions. Thus the dolphin, at the end of the seafood
chain, will be an indicator, among others, of the pace at which
we shall prevent the marine vegetation, the natural laboratories
of the sea, from manufacturing hydrogen and all the other
necessary elements for life. We must live from the sea but it
must also live by us. Obviously the general argument would
also apply to the earth the rivers and the air but even if we limit
ourselves to the topic for today the sea, the prospects would
seem frightening enough.

You'll be turning into a ruddy Martian Mira with that
transistor and its antenna glued to your ear.

Well you don't want her to hear the news so what else can I
do when resting, vox humana will always be the best sleeping
pill.

Anything new?

Not in the headlines bad luck, if you'll let me listen I'll tell
you whether you get tucked in somewhere.

They wouldn't tuck us in, if it's not in the headlines it won't
interest us, get up now and relieve Roberto on guard.

You never know, the blackout on the media may mean
they're on to something, there might be a minor detail they'd
think unimportant, though crucial to us, give me a few
minutes.

But the deletions will be irrecoverably lost and then, and
then I shall walk in with my hypotheses. Hypothesis one, the
father of Andromeda would no longer be Thomas de Umfraville, distant descendant via Aix-la-Chappelle of oh my
prophetic soul my uncle I Claudius, but Cepheus King of
Ethiopia. Thus she could be the plagiarized Abyssinian maid

120

striking with two small mallets on the cords of her dulcimer and singing of Mount Abora but transformed, through incomputable imponderables such as cultural models of the mood of the moment, into a sad Somali girl sailing up the Red Sea as a stowaway.

Hypothesis two, Fatima my Folly will not sail up the Red Sea but up the White Nile or Blue, on the sly, a kind of native bateau ivre or ivory boat to be carved out of an elephant's tusk, or more realistically a boat someone will build of short accacia planks, about three feet long, laying them together like bricks and fastening them with long spikes then caulking them inside with papyrus, driving the single steering-oar down through the keel, and setting up the masts of accacia wood, the sails of papyrus. These vessels however will not sail down the Nile without a leading wind but would have to be towed from the banks. The Nile for some mysterious reason due to imponderables will begin to rise at the summer solstice for a hundred days and then will fall again on account of the summer north winds according to some, or, according to others, because the Nile would flow from Ocean, the stream supposedly circling the world. The second hypothesis would seem to be less rational, and somewhat, if I may so put it, of a legendary character.

Hypothesis three. The third theory would seem the most plausible, but at the same time the furthest from the truth. According to this, the waters of the Nile would come from melting snow, but since it must surely flow from Libya through Ethiopia into Egypt, in other words from a very hot climate into a cooler climate, how could it possibly originate in snow? Obviously this theory must be as worthless as the other two. Anyone with his wits about him will find plenty of arguments to prove that snow could not possibly cause the flooding of the Nile. The strongest would be provided by the winds, blowing hot from those regions. Secondly, the rain will always fall within five days after snow, so that if there were snow there would necessarily be rain too, yet those regions do not know rain or frost. Thirdly, the natives must be

121

black because of the hot climate. Finally, kites and swallows will remain all the year, and cranes will migrate there in winter to escape the cold weather in Scythia. But if there were snow, however little, none of these things could possibly be, they would be contrary to reason.

More reasonable than melting hypotheses would be that Fatima my Folly should eventually reach the Palestinians by spaceship of the desert and fight by their side if she can sort out the reasonable from the unreasonable factions. Since the factions themselves will be unable to do this it may take a long time. The pace of repetition in face-saving formulas and names will accelerate with the speed of the rush through self-consuming history so that all political names will become wrong then right though not all at the same time then wrong again then right which will be wrong or left which will be right left of the extreme centre. This will be very confusing for poor Fatima my Folly who will simply want to die for a noble cause in the name of a lost love. Perhaps she will find a socialist with a human face or a capitalist with a heart of milk and honey to disguide her through the network maze of ways and means.

Dear Ethel,
I hope you will like this postcard of the village and accept it as peace token.

Yours sincerely,
Emma.

122

That would be satisfying, if I were allowed to write, though certainly unwise, provoking more unclear missiles this side of the bowstring demarcation line like a boomerang, or maybe she'll go through a sado-dramatic pretence of not knowing any Emma in order to show forgetful distance until suddenly would come the dawn and the unclear missiles.

Dear Mrs Grant,
I must apologise for not answering your very kind letter sooner. I will spare you the detail of banal though true excuses such as overwork, problems and time passing too quickly, because the underlying reason, as you in your wisdom will surely know, would probably rather be the food for thought in your letter.

With friends there should never be any problem of overfulfilling roles or underassuming responsibilities since friendship by definition should include the giving and the taking of counsel and opinion and even of gentle criticism, such as yours for instance.

But people in tension of love or insufficient love or lovehate, rather like nations, for some mysterious reasons and the imponderables of cultural models oh hell if I have to go off on that groove again my kindest regards will not pass the censoring eye of Hans who will suspect a code, and even if they should prove as sincerely pompous to Orion my efforts will not bear fruit, for when the king of Egypt, pursuing his deserting garrison into Ethiopia, will try to dissuade them from abandoning their wives and children and the gods of their native land, one of the soldiers will point to his private parts and say that wherever those might be there would be no lack of wives and children. And as to gods these will not be mentioned but presumably they would be carried in the same baggage, like parents in a lump of myrrh, which would explain the Egyptian origin of Dionysos and the continuing migration of ideologies in a south-north dialogue of hyper-notions zigzagging across the east-west motion of civilizations which like cities will grow ever westwards, presumably one day biting their own oriental tales. Hence the amazing maze of ways and means.

Soon there will come the expected letter in burotechnish that will make me definitely redundant beyond the shudder of a doubt with the burotechnic explanations as to why I should not after all be entitled to severance pay or perhaps leaving me a dangling hope in burocrastinese.

And I shall go the job-centre where the brawny, balding bastion-bellied, bankrupt little business man in oddly enough electronics will also be queuing, waiting for me eagerly in a great empathy of redundance, hoping to push his cumbersome way into my life with cumbersome jokes about the dole-queue as the answer to an adman's prayer. What adman? I'll ask stupidly and he'll hoveringly explain. Small ads! But why should I be shocked at professional gent late forties divorced looking for lady similar interests and not at a straight pickup in a dole-queue or a phone-in call to Our Lady of Dolors? What will similar interests mean I'll ask conversationally, well everything, except of course physics and electronics, women will never make good scientists and so on, and I shall feel not irritation yet but a foolish flutter of excitement at fraternizing, however briefly, with an element, however itself redundant, of the very force that will make my qualifications not to mention lifelong passions more obsolete than ever, you mustn't worry he'll say and squeeze my hand.

Soon the brain will take off, to the other side of its own mare internum and all the cyclonic warnings of discarded discourses will pass into the autonomous system, racing round on their multiplex business transmitting secret information, irrecoverably deleted.

So that Wallace will continue quite sexplicitly in queues and over snacks in coffeebars to exchange his ponderous advice for a place in my life, which could so easily mean that for the duration of his desire I'll have no life but his, the more unprepossessing the more prepossessive perhaps, playing genuinely enough the good man hard to find but do I want a good man or a man at all and would goodness even if true be enough? A man-a-miracle my friends will exclaim who might see me with him and my smile will be a secret simile or a cheshiregrin yet I'll as slavishly flash inside myself a scientist! At last some knowledgeable talks around say, the small number of constants in the equations at the base of all material behaviour, and if their values were but minimally altered stars wouldn't form would that be true? He'll marvel at my interest but won't reply, and as inappropriately dig up his school anthology to copy out and send La Belle Dame Sans Merci who'll hath him in thrall as in earlier courtships no doubt but elvinly I'll respond with Merci and as in earlier courtships Vixi Puellis or they that'll flee from me which he won't believe or maybe won't receive as text, the seagull flying backwards, the peacock phase, the peahen daring to pretend to a small feather of the peacocktail how exciting.

In a white village of some unpromised land a group of soldiers will advance cautiously with mine-detectors. Behind them, others will be searching derelict houses, machine-gun at the ready. A body. Careful, it may be a booby-trap. Okay, turn him over. Well, well, black moslem, could be. Dead, sergeant. Right, get him out of here. Oh. What now? He may be alive sergeant. Well don't just crouch there, get a stretcher, no wait, I'll call up the ambulance.

A kid. Bad shoulder-wound, doc. Cut the battledress. Jumping Jesus. Cut the shirt. A girl. A tall nubile Nubian, what on earth? Damn good-looking too. Hey, sergeant, could you inform the lieutenant. Careful now. Give her an injection in case she comes to, and clean the wound, I'll have to explore it and dig out the hardware, could be too near the heart to take risks. Any other wounded?

The company will settle its temporary quarters in the village. The captain will pour over a map, the lieutenant will organize the sickbay in one of the houses, the medic will medicate, the patrolmen will rest and eat. Night will fall like a sudden curtain.

Lieutenant, I'll need someone to watch the wounded, we must get some sleep sir.

125

How many wounded doc? My men will need rest too.

About a dozen, but several difficult ops sir, in the worst conditions. They'll all be okay though, there'll be nothing to do but doze watchfully, give sips of water, change a couple of feed-bottles, give pee-bottles and call me if anything untoward should occur.

Well all right, I'll find someone. Sergeant.

Sir.

Anyone we could detail for sickbay watch?

I'll see sir. Er, how about that young civvy?

Might be a good idea. He might as well earn his keep, he shouldn't be here at all, it'd be considered most irregular by anyone but the captain, some damn kinsman of his, wanting a looksee, though I shouldn't say so. Budding journalist I shouldn't wonder, unwilling to work up the normal way.

He'd seem more like a wandering bum to me sir if you'll pardon the hexpression. Oo'd be out for kicks.

No sergeant, you must first admit he couldn't be less of a burden as orderly, cook, learning first aid, even how to handle a gun.

And a mine-detector sir.

What!

Yes sir. In secret like, then joining the group on the q.t. this morning, and afterwards, well what can I do, he ain't under orders and don't do nothing badly and don't care anyways. If you ask me sir he'll ave the death-wish on him, one of them mystical nye-ilists or something, or else he'd be a budding terrorist, learning his trade for free.

Hmmm. Well, keep an eye on him, but meanwhile pack him off to sickbay.

And Wally, who blessedly will have nothing to bargain but his name, his downandoutedness and his optimism in exchange for mine and my scepticism, will to my astonishment offer precisely that, making his insistent proposals every day by phone by letter by constant presence, declaring eternal and tender love without the shudder of a doubt as to my longing for just such a signal honour, talking of my emotional desert and assuming a wilish game of playing hard to get instead of a companionly desire to know about emergent properties that should be objectively describable unlike conscious thought and therefore unfeminine until his forming passion turn me captive pooling our resources on a small pigfarm a super idea your relative bankloan my relative brawn your craftswoman-ship, my handymanship our brains our courage our love.

Shall I once more have to pretend to be terrified of electricity, unable to change a light-switch, and mimecstatic at his doing so? Some gulls will even fly backwards to impress their females, and so some girls not to depress their males.

The budding terrorist, who'll look about eighteen, will be very suntanned and dark-haired, appearing neither middle-eastern nor middle-western of any faction. He will speak French and English and smatter Arabic and be suspected by all, but he'll also have an insolent assurance weirdly admixtured with soft charm and a disarming smile, which will make suspicion cohabit with protectiveness. He will stroll along to sickbay and willingly tend the wounded. Please. Me die. Allow, the sad Somali girl will say in smattered Arabic.

Shsh. Sleep. Well soon.

Like die.

Water?

Die.

Take. Drink. Little.

Mmm. My friend?

Where your friend? Who?

You. Mustapha?

No. Not Mustapha.

Ah. You Mussa?

No. Not Mussa.

No. Mussa speak me-language.

What you-language?

Mussa dead. Me like die.

No. Not die. Sleep.

You. Speak you-language?

No, Arabic not me-language. Try, like you.

Is not you-language?
No, me-language English.
English. Somali some English. Arabic for Koran.
You. Somali?
Somali.
What you do here?
Long. Long. Desert. Camel. Hills. Feet. Boat. Big big motors. Hide.
Sleep.
No. Wake. What you do?
Look you. Beautiful.
Me? Beautiful?
Like Song of Songs.
Mussa. Ow.
Not move. Still. Wound.
Me will fight.
Sleep now.
What you name?
Roland.
Wolan?
Rro–lan–do.
Rro–lan–do. Wolan. Me Fatima. You Wolan.
You Fatima. Me Wolan.
You fight?
No, peace. United Nations.
Nations? Unite? What nations?
Later. Tell. Sleep now.
Sleep. First tell. How peace?
Sweep. Mines. Street.
Sweep? Street?
Later. Fatima. Beautiful Fatima. Sleep. Please.
Sleep.
We must err on the side of caution will say my knight-errant, about the loan, not love, for he will with trousers belted beneath his enormous belly barge in beyond the shutter of a doubt into my life and couldn't err on any side of any stepping stones into the dark. Wouldn't just one wrong pole if

128

discovered in a far galaxy annul the very possibility of formulating the basic equations and so collapse the entire paradigm? Wouldn't he agree about hopeless sense distortion so that all we should hope for would be precise description, like blind men groping? No he would not. Surely I wouldn't question now, he'll say as to a child, the roundness of the earth? How would that be for a conversation-stopper? But I could imagine others, and they will surely come, you humanists for instance, don't extrapolate, in answer to my inquiry about not inquiring about the route of an electron from one point to another since any such knowledge might prevent it from ever reaching the other point. There'll be no bridges to take even when I'll get to them, let alone stepping-stones.

And so my other sidekick will apparently be not Apollo or even Pseudo-Dionysos but Silenus. Not someone who'll bargain his help, that'll be a relief to owe no gratitude for helpful demolition, but whom I'll have to help, that should please the moral imps, and a great tenderness for his very clownishness will invade me with the surprisingly over-whelming force of a love-discourse out of the middle-ages to some princesse lointaine, waking ancient structures that will make me try very hard to want to be pygmalioned, even though for that it will be necessary to go on seeming really idiotic to prop the pigmylion. To die, to sleep — no more, and by a sleep to say we end the heart-ache and the thousand natural shocks — What would that be from?

There'll be a pause. I must I will not show my thousand natural shocks at these deep double-cultural gulfs, why should I, he wouldn't feel a qualm at my not understanding about not knowing about the route of an electron, the more tolerant him. I wouldn't denigrate it though, I couldn't, even without playing idiotic. He'll be used, he'll say, to being surrounded with non-scientists and thus not discussing these things. The detail I'll say, of course, but the implications, the philosophy of it, surely everyone should be passionately interested? He'll shrug as if to say I wouldn't understand, and suddenly look

129

very lonely.

So your dropping out of scientific circles I'll say gently would be particularly hard for you?

He'll shrug again. Yes, he'll suppose so. Then with his ho-ho laugh but why cry over spilt atoms and I'll laugh too and he'll insist again, we must look to our future together, you, the love of my life and so on. But Wally we'll have to have something in common surely, what shall we talk about when we'll stop talking about love? My love I'll never believe the day will come when we'll have nothing to say, why if we love each other we should never stop talking! Why pin it all on intellectual exchange?

It'll be a very good question, but if there could at least be exchange it might be fun for a while providing he doesn't atomize not only my inquiries, which I'll have to stop, but my own lifelong passions multitudinous, from astronomy to Zeus from Borges to Yggdrasil from choreography to xylophones from Dante to the Wits from ethnology to Vitruvius from fiction to utopias from grammatology to theororism from heresies to sestinas from ideograms to rhetoric from jazz to quatrocento from Kierkegaard to Plotinus from Lear to Oedipus from mimesis to aporia to nihilism, he may dyscognize them all and all the others out of his epistemes.

Wouldn't it be better to make up a story in my head unheeded, with characters talking, a government source will say, a military source will announce Mr Fitzjohn, Captain Sir.

Right sergeant, bring him in.

Look what is this? You can't put me on a charge, I'll never join any army.

All right sergeant you may go. Now look here young man, you can't have it both ways. You must know very well you'd have no right to be here at all were it not for my admitting you unofficially, for the, erm, experience, to please your cousin, and it should be quite clear, on the one hand, that it couldn't be as a soldier but as an odd job man, to relieve the real soldiers under pressure from some of the chores, and that therefore you should not carry out any soldiering duties whatsoever, we're not in Ruritania.

But —

Don't interrupt. And, on the other hand, that this arrangement would be entirely unofficial, that we would as it were close our eyes, but on condition that you obey orders. What do you suppose would happen to me if you got blown up?

How can I get blown up with a mine-detector in front of me?

Don't be childish. It ought to be clear to you that if you voluntarily enter into any organization, of whatever nature and in whatever capacity, you must accept its rules even if not officially part of it. Therefore I must advise you, indeed order you, to consider yourself under army discipline as long as this unit will tolerate you in its midst. I should have thought that wouldn't need saying.

Why say it then? Have you ever heard of my disobeying an order?

Not a direct order Fitzjohn, but a general commonsense injunction, an implicit agreement. However, I will recognize my responsibility in this, erm, merely to oblige your cousin, a good friend of mine. As you may be aware, I do not speak to you as a commanding officer would speak to a private, who'd never be so insolent, and in a sense you'd be well below the humblest of my soldiers, but as an officer to a civilian, or as a father to a young scatterbrain. And I will recognize also that until this ridiculous escapade, well, let's say no more about it but you must keep your good record clean. I believe, let me see, you'll be doing extra fatigue in sickbay again tonight?

Yes. Sir.

Well you'll be tired, go and get some sleep. And if I hear any more nonsense out of you, off you'll go to Headquarters with a report, I'd send you now but I can't spare an escort.

Oh I wouldn't need an escort. Sir.

Of course you would young man, we couldn't have you wandering around or hitching rides in battle territory where we should officially be keeping the peace, you'd either get shot or cause a diplomatic incident. Now off with you, and

131

consider yourself lucky.

Yes. Sir. Thank you — er — please, sir.

Now what?

Could I perhaps stay on sickbay duty from now on?

Well if they need you there more than elsewhere it wouldn't be a bad idea, you'll have to see the M. O., you mustn't cause him any trouble either, then check with the sergeant. Dismiss.

After which regular dressing-down Roland will dress wounds as unofficial medical orderly of a low-grade kind, assisting mostly in menial tasks such as washing and feeding the sick, emptying their detritus and keeping the place scrupulously clean. Fortunately for the lack of a female bedpan Fatima will soon be up, and after a week the dozen or so wounded and their unofficial orderly will be escorted back to Headquarters with a note from the Captain as to the irregularity of one wounded and one orderly. The young man, Fitzjohn, an Englishman, would have walked in from nowhere and offered his services in sickbay. Would Headquarters deal as they'd see fit with both the boy Fitzjohn and the girl patient. The latter would seem, according to Fitzjohn, to come from Somali, and to be therefore of the Hamitic race, but this should no doubt be investigated before repatriation.

The answer could also be a sudden sympathy of redundance, even if it may soon become a redundant sympathy, for him as one of the few technoscientists to be themselves overtaken in their unbusinesslike complacency by the disbelievable speed of their own development, and for myself as one of the many humanists to be cocooned in the suspension of their disbelief by the slow centuries of civilization. You mustn't worry he'll say and squeeze my hand.

On the gold market the ingot will probably fall by eighty pounds if the dollar continues on its record climb vot ze hell Mira you muss zat sing out svitch, it vill you on duty to sleep bringen, aber it vill ze prisoner vielen Tagen back set, Dummkopf.

Okay Gisela. Though apparently she won't change in any

way. Nor for that matter will the market, inflating or deflating as usual, I doubt whether it will be in the least affected.

How vould you know, du Literatur-Kreatur?

I wouldn't, except for the droning tone, no panic. How long do you think they'll hold out?

For ever dear guardians, for ever, beyond all your for-ever-to-be-postponed ultimatums, you'll achieve nothing through mere ideology as you should know, touching though your innocence may pip-pip-pip.

Sei still! Und genough of your bluff. Und du Mira —

Shsh listen to this, rumours from police headquarters that an arrest will be made any minute in connection with the kidnapping. Our special correspondent at Scotland Yard will tell us what to think of it Jack Newman can you hear me? Jack?

Dummkopf Mira svitch down!

Okay okay small technical problem but we'll bring you Jack Newman in a few moments meanwhile, here in the studio we'll be able to question Mr John Briggs our financial expert from Jack Newman? Ah. Do you hear me? Yes Paul, well, with due caution mind, an arrest may be imminent. The man in question would seem to be a certain professor, er, Albi-reo, Cygnus, an eminently respectable academic who, according to certain police sources who shall be nameless would apparently have master-minded the whole operation would that be correct Inspector? Really I don't know where you'd get that kind of information, if an arrest were imminent we would not announce it beforehand to the press. I wish you journalists would observe the pact of silence and let us get on with our job. So you would deny the rumour? Emphatically. Thank you Inspector, well as you may imagine Paul it won't be easy to get any information down here. Okay Jack well stick around if they'll let you and of course you'll have priority if any more should come through. Perhaps Mr Briggs, our financial expert, could tell us what to think of it? Could you enlighten us Mr Briggs?

Well, point-blank like this I couldn't really say much, except that this whole affair would seem quite inscrutably silly, if not

133

a mere eccentric incident, if a human life, of an important statesperson, were not at stake, and in any case we shouldn't come to premature conclusions at this stage.

Quite. But do you know this Professor, er, Cygnus?

Well, let me see.

Paul? Paul? Something may be about to happen, a black maria will be coming into the gates any second now but of course it could be routine if it weren't for the very large body of police, wait, just a second, now get back there, no, no interviews now get back sir will you, can you tell me who, no, get back, yes, tell the world I'll prove my innocence tell them my name Albireo Cygnus Professor of now will you get back we'll make an official statement in due course when we'll be ready, you wouldn't want to throw the suspicion of publicity on a man before that would you? Paul? Yes, yes, congratulations Paul a scoop but you'd better obey the guardians of the law and stay out of trouble, ring us back as soon as you get more details, official or unofficial okay? I trust listeners will excuse all that noise and confusion and be glad of this extraordinary information which we shall now try and sort out for you, though we won't be able to deal with it just yet as more than a live item, a surprise for us as it will be for you. Now Mr Briggs would you be able to recollect this man Professor er Cygnus?

A crank I believe, but a harmless one I should think, I couldn't imagine, well, I'd be loath to prejudge him at this stage.

Quite. But wouldn't it be a little surprising, after the former rumours of a German woman master-minding the whole operation, to find an apparently respectable English professor arrested?

If you don't mind, I should be commenting here on the financial aspects of this affair, not on the police side, with which I could hardly be expected to be conversant.

Of course, please excuse me Mr Briggs, with all the excitement.

Precisely, this whole affair will prove once again that

excitement will get us nowhere. The City and all financial centres will continue to keep calm and thus recuperate with perfect ease from this very minor initial shock, as indeed we always shall.

Okay, svitch avay Mira zis Schwachsinnigkeit no more ve vant, sehmal ze prisoner sie vill for lange upon it live.

Could you really be the master-mind, Gisela?

Du muss mind your biznis.

Further news may come in any moment and we shall of course interrupt the programmes as soon as we receive new information and we'll all go on as if.

As if, for instance, I were someone else, really interested beyond casual interchange and kindness in the kindly creature who with his raincoat and jacket creased and either mis-buttoned or open to the winds his trousers belted beneath his enormous belly and falling on his ankles will barge into my life like a flapping scarecrow, expressing his sheer enchantment at finding me, despite my talent and intelligence, so marvellously feminine.

If we were people in a nineteenth-century novel I could cruelly send him packing, like Emma Mr Elton, but today when women's very freedom will be turned against them by even moderately clever men I may incredibly have to go through the ludicrous motions of being immensely flattered by old myths under new names, and of reciprocating to the same degree, the repressed prodigal returning once again on pain of abnormal syndromes. So that I'll be, for only a while let's hope, a grateful substitute small ad response to an enthusiastic substitute small ad.

Fatima, me tell. Me not sweep mines.

No. Wolan sweep street. House, sweep. Not long.

No, Fatima. Me will finish sweep. Will go far. India.

India?

East. But Africa also. Will go with Fatima protect to Somali.

Fatima will not to Somali.

Fatima hear. Important. Fatima will in hospital. Not Wolan.

135

Not Wolan?

Not permit. Fatima well after. Fatima they will send to Somali.

Me will not to Somali. Me will fight, will die.

You not say this to white man.

Me will go with Wolan. Wolan tell me world.

Me protect Fatima.

Yes. Fatima will good wife. Will accept protect.

All my objections, which I'll put as genuine unaccept-abilities of my cassandring person, which no man'll take, will be swept under his magic carpet with the ho-ho joke if no man will and I will, what am I? Go in peace! *Vale!*

And with my sidetrack mind I'll disguide my amazement by half inventing for him my invading respect for his lack of complication. Truly I'll be sorely tempted unless sorely truly tempted, for what will be the use of humanist understanding in the featureless future, and yet I'll know it'll be he who'll end up cassandring me, precisely in nomansland where the male gods will ever take over the pythian oracles, turning them into twittering spokespersons. My very happiness without him, to be so besieged, will soon be blackmarked against me as pretentiousness, as would even now any quietly voiced hint that life with him might be more limited than life with colleagues or even pigs and magic stepping-stones. No doubt the agenda will also include some face-saving device like let us recognize one another before annihilating one another. Sandra my love of course I will he'll exclaim and I'll love you even more, if that were possible, when you'll be truly out of the university and wholly mine, when thanks to this extra-ordinary chance to remake your life with me you will accept, and face, being only a woman.

A polar low will sneak down the coast depositing snow everywhere.

Soon the ecopsychic system will crumble, and sado-experts will fly in from everywhere and poke into its entrails and make soothing unsoothsayings and we'll all go on as if.

Roland, after explanations involving only his own foolhardiness, will be told to stand by for an escort to the nearest British Consulate. That night he will quietly infiltrate into the hospital and swiftly sweep from ward to ward, skilfully avoiding the night staff and looking at each bed, switching on a torch for one split second. Luck will be with him for he will find her soon, put his hand on her mouth and wake her gently, lighting his own face and beckoning within the beam. She will get up at once and follow him. Outside he will lead her to a bomb-shelter and take a pair of jeans and a shirt from behind a pile of sandbags. She will remove the regulation nightwear, unashamed in the halfdark, and don the shirt and jeans. They will move out of the city together, on an early bus, and hide in a waiting lorry on the outskirts.

Oh they will go far those two, the princess Fatima my Folly of the evasive eyes and the Rolandrover streetsweeper Anon, sweeping the dragon's tail of sibylisation.

The problem of automation, Wally my new Amalgamemnon will very slowly bring out with apparently painful concentration in the dole-queue, will be what to do with the totally brainless, even streetsweeping could be done mechanically. Perhaps, I might say, a whole series of jobs but no, I would not reply since some brains such as mine will now be as redundant as some brawn, unless to be recycled into a text processor at some future date we must hold back or forth as long as possible.

Meanwhile my uncle Ego, elbowdeep in blood and placenta, must in his floodlights plunge into the entrails of the placid unmuscular whale to extract the blocked profoetus of my freedom which I would have forgotten to feed. Perhaps I should walk dishevelled the battlements of Troy uttering prophecies from time to time unheeded. Perhaps I should allow myself to be abducted by a band of terrorists who will hold me prisoner in Oblitopia or why not right here?

Tonight over a vast meal I shall have cooked for his vaster belly Wally will search the dessicated madlanes of the early century and put in his thumb and pull out a plum the non-creativity of women, and Jews, and blacks, brilliant per-formers yes but lacking in the true creative spirit, though Jews would on the contrary have it in physics which would prove purely racial differences in genius and ungenius, and I shall put on my postface and mimagree, unless I put on my preface and go through the routine, would you contest Science, he'll ask with the whole weight of his ponderous person on the word, and the reports of geneticians on differences not due to environment? Whose reports? What fun his eyes sexclaiming as if disputation were proof of my commitment. Or else annoyed, already, at being disputed, reminding me again as if by chance of my emotional desert and his irrigation of it as over-signaled honour and I shall perhaps murmur a garden briefly untended rather but who will be deceiving whom on that particular playground?

My substitute lover as he will jocularly name it will murmur to me about mulching potatoes in Peru and yams in Nigeria and cabbages in the Caribbean, keeping the earth cool for a much better crop and in Nigeria making the building of the hillocks quite unnecessary. Or perhaps you will take industrial action or will you accept the arbitration body?

Far in a dehauntological campaign from zone to zone, zig-zagging north and south, east and west, the lovers will wander from Sidon to Damascus from Antioch to Phocaea and Troy, from Byzantium to Babylon and up to Nineveh and down again to Susa, finding a sort of wisdom and a sort of love. She will teach him Somali through arabesques, he will teach her the world, with childlike analogies of tribal warfare or village rivalries or the jealousies of men, just imagine tribes, Fatima, only hundreds and hundreds of times bigger, bigger than from Somali to Syria, each country like a violent boy fighting for

138

the possession of a girl called Fortune, each country regroup-
ing itself with others not for peace but for strength and power
and raw materials, so that you'll get huge blocks, all trying to
buy and bully the smaller countries and to make them fight
each other and weaken them. And inside each country, small
or big, there'll be different tribes belonging to one of the big
blocks, they'll be paid by them and given guns and adopt their
gods. So that no group will remain loyal and whole for long, it
will split into small groups, more and more splits, until you
get all the way back to tribal warfare again. Do you understand, Fatima? The story of the world moving backwards in a
way, and Fatima will teach him gently, shyly, with evasive
eyes and arabesques, how really to love a woman.

They will hide and hike, smile and sweep and cook and clean
and help to feed and firstaid the starving and fetch and carry
their way across deserts and seas, in the steps of conquerors,
down the Tigris and the Euphrates and following Darius and
Alexander and Marco Polo towards Ghenghis Khan, to Kabul
and Katmandu and Kuala Lumpur, to Kampuchea and
Kazakhstan and Nanking and Hong Kong, passing as if by
magic through tyrannies massacres bomb outrages revolutions occupations famines invasions earthquakes floods
uncivil wars, casting spells upon frontier guards ticket-
collectors soldiers and officials and spells of kindness on cart-
drivers beggars rice-growers and bridge-builders. He shall tell
her tales of Tyre and Sidon and the Phoenician empire, of
Helen and the Trojan horse, of Croesus the Lydian attacking a
great empire and bringing down his own, of Cambyses in
Egypt sending spies into Ethiopia, of Cyrus, Darius, Xerxes,
tales of the rise and fall of all empires from the Assyrian to the
American Russian Chinese. She will sing him talisman tales of
love and legend tatooed with halftold taboos of tenderness and
ancient proverbs like lick me now will say the salt.

And I shall spend much time picking up Wally's clothes
strewn anyhow over the floor and hanging up his creased
trousers and shirts. But my envious respect for his lack of
complication will filter growing guineaworms of distaste for a

multitude of self-indulgences physiological intellectual and aesthetic as against my natural preferences for, say, early patristic sensual modes, my anchoretish desert he will also call first tenderly then angrily my ivory tower. So that once voiced these preferences to be offered generously as complementaries, in other words to be yielded up, will under his no doubt rightly mocking demolition of them yield again to the truer explanation of a cynical exchange on either side of a little affection and funtrips finding a tumbledown farm, tiny, making it in our minds as others would make a child.

Dear Miss Inkytie, I'd be tickled that you should think you might get away with a pretence at peace-making while at the same time ironically signing it Emma, and she'll add that it will have taken her days to fathom that one out but the handwriting so dreadfully familiar from her essays will have given the game away and so on and so forth for pages ending with a dire warning against trusting that dreadful and vulgar little man, so obviously a sponger, need she spell it out, this would be positively the last time and she'd probably be dead right.

I wish I could go back to school and teach the history of the future the geography of effaceable memory the botany of trees you can't see for the woods and how to write on sand, count on nothing and read bubbles. I could speak to an issue with a tissue of lies like wavetroughs tunnel ends and silver linings and get rhapsodes on the knuckles. And when the powder of instant history will scatter to the winds in Oblitopia, what shall we do with all the unbiodegradable tapes and reels and floppy disks and databank chips and instant archives of discompromisecourse? If we burn them all they will pollute the atmostfearic density, stifle the forests and cornfields and if we don't they will get entangled in the branches of the trees we won't see for the woods and in the teeth of tractotalitarian jaws, clutter the seas, darken the air, cling to giant tankers like giant seaweed octopuses, wrap themselves round jetengines in a death embrace. The planet will ooze dead history like guineaworms out of its closed eyes. Unless history simply reverse itself, shrinking back into its own tail to lash out at the last and kill the goose that'll lay the golden ages.

At least you'll have to admit that a war between England and Germany would now be inconceivable, Amalgememnon will say at dinner, or some such irrefutable item he will present as highly controversial before the rest of the routine the washing up the undressing the chucking me under the breast with a cluck of his palate on the way to the john. Tomorrow at breakfast I may try another break-feast attempt and with incredulity hear his ears click shut despite the studied zeal he'll use to catch the air-filling trivia, excuse me he'll say during the dish-clattering or the tap-running, could you repeat? And when I shall at last succeed in leaving him it will remain a mystery how anyone so highly trained in physics and so physically solid could seem to lack a whole dimension of being, or will it only be for me and therefore my own dimension that I won't have given him because he will so very quickly have stripped me of it? Or vice versa for that'll surely be what he'll think of me and no doubt he'd be right, like everybody else.

Meanwhile he'll speak without thinking and I'll think without speaking but never quite together since my speaking to any purpose but pub platitudes will already make him angry. And just as the young Scythians will be unable to learn the language of the Amazons but the women will pick up theirs and therefore disappear, so he will dispossess me of my friends, my activities, my reading and even frown on my desire for a television set, a glance at the evening paper should be enough he'll say, at least one may in theory verify. Verify what, the sources or the inner consistency from page to page? So I'll have my lover substitute who'll be a climatologist forecasting both an ice-age and a warming up through the greenhouse effect of pollution but not at the same time and the interviewer will keenly pounce exactly like Wally with repeated questions about having it both ways, both can't be true. But then, will the long term or the short term fuse or fiss?

Wally won't answer that either or even speculate. Surely with his falling trousers he'd be more convincing and even

141

more comfortable in a Tudor period wearing doublet and hose, a Falstaff without Shakespeare's verbal art or Verdi's melodic grandeur. But perhaps we should both retire to the age of dinosaurs and other extinct creatures. Wouldn't it be better to stop playing hard to keep for a good man hard to find, who when the wooing pressure will have gone the way of all sales patter will cease to be the warrior of my rest and interest and merely want me to be always there, like now, like him, but not so slovenly slipslop slippershod naturally. Why don't you have television he will say then and I'll reply perhaps to avoid dictators but only to make him say how pretentious and so forth.

Yet none of my private telematics will interest him why have private telematics his attitude will say when you could have only me and it would be a very good question if I could think of an answer as to which would be fleshierbloodier among shadow-figures, the simulacra Venus will abuse all lovers with or Cassandra Emma Vautrin Malvolio Fabrice Criseyde Europe Faust Milly Theale Sancho Panza Captain Ahab Smerdiakov Pierre Menard Herzog or Wally, he'll dyscognize them all in his hohomonologue you humanists he'll say and no doubt rightly with your pretentious and obsolete culture why, you wouldn't even bother to understand the inside of an electric switch. Then teach me show me I'll pretend but he'll predefer to keep that mystery to himself, nor shall I bother to riposte about bothering to understand his own short-circuiting of his own dream-desire.

That will leave cuisine preferably rich to talk about and current affairs preferably through the distancing blurring telescope of the dismal bunch of rightists so I'll have to cook a great deal and quote my lover substitute for him to comment less well or drop him, but drop him he won't let me without drama please don't leave me he'll beg I'll do anything, anything you'll ask. Except what I should ask, to recognize me I'll murmur unheard and so I'll try to share at least my interest in modern minstrelsy, that surely will be unpretentious and unobsolete but no, pop will be for adolescents and women,

142

not a manly thing. I'll play along a while, not quite knowing why, perhaps to see how often, always, he'll accept money to help him out or let me pay, he doing the fumbling, or if he'll ever, never, refuse and how soon, soon, he'll be unable to keep up the love-patter as object of exchange. What will he do when he'll know I'll receive no severance money at all? Will my pretence have become almost real and outlast his? If not I'll have as usual to behave real bad in other words reproach him so as to let him drop me as impossible. Neutrally possible Cabinet sources will refuse to comment.

And yet, nothing will ever be exactly as the twittering dove will see it in retrospect one day from her relentlessly pursued advantage that she won't have in the intellectual infrastructure or arsehole of posterity, where she will sweep up the godshit among a dismal bunch of performing seals flapping their disguideologies unknown to themselves at low altitudes right to the left of centre, their small ears clicking shut at any change in the atmostfearic density around split human hairs to be beaten up with the whites of our eyes and added to the mixtake as before. Speak softly to her nervous system and she will loveinbloom as a poppycockcrow.

Soon he will come. Soon he will sleep and snore, a foreign body in bed. There will occur the blanket bodily transfer to the livingroom for a night of utterly other discourses that will spark out of a minicircus of light upon a page of say Lucretius and generate endless stepping-stones into the dark, gathering up solitude as a needed strength that will nevertheless be resented by one and all especially one.

As if such solitudinous strength were not a newly developing organ of survival in these gregarious solitudinous times when men and women of all ages and abilities may suddenly be deprived not only of a living wage but of a lifelong's loving stage.

Tomorrow at breakfast he will talk of this and that and then we shall walk down the street to the Job-Centre as usual. I could use my savings and severance money to make a humble down payment on a tumbledown tiny farm to keep hens and pigs and rabbits or something and live on leeks and cabbages, but Wally my Amalgamemnon will have eaten up my savings and the State my other Amalgamenon will not give me severance pay. Swing low, sweet chariot.

Wouldn't it be better to make up a story in my head unheeded and unhinged, with characters talking, a government source will say, a scientific source will argue (the source will say), we shall soon live exciting times. The characters should also include spokespersons, statespersons, handypersons, highwaypersons and wifpersons who will perhaps indulge in the secret vice of reading redundant textual sources of redundant psychic sources in redundant humanist animals, thus putting spokes and states and highways into their wheelchairs and careering around in their nomansland. Secret cabinet sources will refuse to comment on these shadow-figures and I shall mimagree, how should I not?

Paris, 1983.

CHRISTINE BROOKE-ROSE was born in Geneva, Switzerland in 1923. She was raised in Brussels and educated at Somerville College, Oxford, and University College, London. During World War II, Brooke-Rose served as an intelligence officer in the British Women's Auxiliary Air Force, working at Bletchley Park.

She began writing in 1956. Her first two novels, *The Languages of Love* (1957) and *The Sycamore Tree* (1958), were satirical novels of manners. From 1956 to 1968, Brooke-Rose worked in London as a freelance literary journalist. In 1968, she moved to Paris, beginning a career as a teacher of Anglo-American literature and literary theory at the University of Paris. She is the author of over a dozen books, among which are *Xorandor* (1986), *Verbivore* (1990), and *Textermination* (1991).

Petros Abatzoglou, *What Does Mrs. Freeman Want?*
Michal Ajvaz, *The Golden Age.*
The Other City.
Pierre Albert-Birot, *Grabinoulor.*
Yuz Aleshkovsky, *Kangaroo.*
Felipe Alfau, *Chromos.*
Locos.
Ivan Ângelo, *The Celebration.*
The Tower of Glass.
David Antin, *Talking.*
António Lobo Antunes, *Knowledge of Hell.*
Alain Arias-Misson, *Theatre of Incest.*
John Ashbery and James Schuyler, *A Nest of Ninnies.*
Heimrad Bäcker, *transcript.*
Djuna Barnes, *Ladies Almanack.*
Ryder.
John Barth, *LETTERS.*
Sabbatical.
Donald Barthelme, *The King.*
Paradise.
Svetislav Basara, *Chinese Letter.*
Mark Binelli, *Sacco and Vanzetti Must Die!*
Andrei Bitov, *Pushkin House.*
Louis Paul Boon, *Chapel Road.*
My Little War.
Summer in Termuren.
Roger Boylan, *Killoyle.*
Ignácio de Loyola Brandão, *Anonymous Celebrity.*
Teeth under the Sun.
Zero.
Bonnie Bremser, *Troia: Mexican Memoirs.*
Christine Brooke-Rose, *Amalgamemnon.*
Brigid Brophy, *In Transit.*
Meredith Brosnan, *Mr. Dynamite.*
Gerald L. Bruns, *Modern Poetry and the Idea of Language.*
Evgeny Bunimovich and J. Kates, eds., *Contemporary Russian Poetry: An Anthology.*
Gabrielle Burton, *Heartbreak Hotel.*
Michel Butor, *Degrees.*
Mobile.
Portrait of the Artist as a Young Ape.
G. Cabrera Infante, *Infante's Inferno.*
Three Trapped Tigers.
Julieta Campos, *The Fear of Losing Eurydice.*
Anne Carson, *Eros the Bittersweet.*
Camilo José Cela, *Christ versus Arizona.*
The Family of Pascual Duarte.
The Hive.
Louis-Ferdinand Céline, *Castle to Castle.*
Conversations with Professor Y.
London Bridge.
Normance.
North.
Rigadoon.
Hugo Charteris, *The Tide Is Right.*
Jerome Charyn, *The Tar Baby.*
Marc Cholodenko, *Mordechai Schamz.*

Joshua Cohen, *Witz.*
Emily Holmes Coleman, *The Shutter of Snow.*
Robert Coover, *A Night at the Movies.*
Stanley Crawford, *Log of the S.S. The Mrs Unguentine.*
Some Instructions to My Wife.
Robert Creeley, *Collected Prose.*
René Crevel, *Putting My Foot in It.*
Ralph Cusack, *Cadenza.*
Susan Daitch, *L.C.*
Storytown.
Nicholas Delbanco, *The Count of Concord.*
Nigel Dennis, *Cards of Identity.*
Peter Dimock, *A Short Rhetoric for Leaving the Family.*
Ariel Dorfman, *Konfidenz.*
Coleman Dowell, *The Houses of Children.*
Island People.
Too Much Flesh and Jabez.
Arkadii Dragomoshchenko, *Dust.*
Rikki Ducornet, *The Complete Butcher's Tales.*
The Fountains of Neptune.
The Jade Cabinet.
The One Marvelous Thing.
Phosphor in Dreamland.
The Stain.
The Word "Desire."
William Eastlake, *The Bamboo Bed.*
Castle Keep.
Lyric of the Circle Heart.
Jean Echenoz, *Chopin's Move.*
Stanley Elkin, *A Bad Man.*
Boswell: A Modern Comedy.
Criers and Kibitzers, Kibitzers and Criers.
The Dick Gibson Show.
The Franchiser.
George Mills.
The Living End.
The MacGuffin.
The Magic Kingdom.
Mrs. Ted Bliss.
The Rabbi of Lud.
Van Gogh's Room at Arles.
Annie Ernaux, *Cleaned Out.*
Lauren Fairbanks, *Muzzle Thyself.*
Sister Carrie.
Leslie A. Fiedler, *Love and Death in the American Novel.*
Juan Filloy, *Op Oloop.*
Gustave Flaubert, *Bouvard and Pécuchet.*
Kass Fleisher, *Talking out of School.*
Ford Madox Ford, *The March of Literature.*
Jon Fosse, *Melancholy.*
Max Frisch, *I'm Not Stiller.*
Man in the Holocene.
Carlos Fuentes, *Christopher Unborn.*
Distant Relations.
Terra Nostra.
Where the Air Is Clear.

JANICE GALLOWAY, *Foreign Parts.*
  The Trick Is to Keep Breathing.
WILLIAM H. GASS, *Cartesian Sonata*
  and Other Novellas.
  Finding a Form.
  A Temple of Texts.
  The Tunnel.
  Willie Masters' Lonesome Wife.
GÉRARD GAVARRY, *Hoppla! 1 2 3.*
ETIENNE GILSON,
  The Arts of the Beautiful.
  Forms and Substances in the Arts.
C. S. GISCOMBE, *Giscome Road.*
  Here.
  Prairie Style.
DOUGLAS GLOVER, *Bad News of the Heart.*
  The Enamoured Knight.
WITOLD GOMBROWICZ,
  A Kind of Testament.
KAREN ELIZABETH GORDON, *The Red Shoes.*
GEORGI GOSPODINOV, *Natural Novel.*
JUAN GOYTISOLO, *Count Julian.*
  Juan the Landless.
  Makbara.
  Marks of Identity.
PATRICK GRAINVILLE, *The Cave of Heaven.*
HENRY GREEN, *Back.*
  Blindness.
  Concluding.
  Doting.
  Nothing.
JIŘÍ GRUŠA, *The Questionnaire.*
GABRIEL GUDDING,
  Rhode Island Notebook.
MELA HARTWIG, *Am I a Redundant*
  Human Being?
JOHN HAWKES, *The Passion Artist.*
  Whistlejacket.
ALEKSANDAR HEMON, ED.,
  Best European Fiction 2010.
AIDAN HIGGINS, *A Bestiary.*
  Balcony of Europe.
  Bornholm Night-Ferry.
  Darkling Plain: Texts for the Air.
  Flotsam and Jetsam.
  Langrishe, Go Down.
  Scenes from a Receding Past.
  Windy Arbours.
ALDOUS HUXLEY, *Antic Hay.*
  Crome Yellow.
  Point Counter Point.
  Those Barren Leaves.
  Time Must Have a Stop.
MIKHAIL IOSSEL AND JEFF PARKER, EDS.,
  Amerika: Russian Writers View the
  United States.
GERT JONKE, *The Distant Sound.*
  Geometric Regional Novel.
  Homage to Czerny.
  The System of Vienna.
JACQUES JOUET, *Mountain R.*
  Savage.
CHARLES JULIET, *Conversations with*
  Samuel Beckett and Bram van
  Velde.
MIEKO KANAI, *The Word Book.*

HUGH KENNER, *The Counterfeiters.*
  Flaubert, Joyce and Beckett:
  The Stoic Comedians.
  Joyce's Voices.
DANILO KIŠ, *Garden, Ashes.*
  A Tomb for Boris Davidovich.
ANITA KONKKA, *A Fool's Paradise.*
GEORGE KONRÁD, *The City Builder.*
TADEUSZ KONWICKI, *A Minor Apocalypse.*
  The Polish Complex.
MENIS KOUMANDAREAS, *Koula.*
ELAINE KRAF, *The Princess of 72nd Street.*
JIM KRUSOE, *Iceland.*
EWA KURYLUK, *Century 21.*
ERIC LAURRENT, *Do Not Touch.*
VIOLETTE LEDUC, *La Bâtarde.*
SUZANNE JILL LEVINE, *The Subversive*
  Scribe: Translating Latin
  American Fiction.
DEBORAH LEVY, *Billy and Girl.*
  Pillow Talk in Europe and Other
  Places.
JOSÉ LEZAMA LIMA, *Paradiso.*
ROSA LIKSOM, *Dark Paradise.*
OSMAN LINS, *Avalovara.*
  The Queen of the Prisons of Greece.
ALF MAC LOCHLAINN,
  The Corpus in the Library.
  Out of Focus.
RON LOEWINSOHN, *Magnetic Field(s).*
BRIAN LYNCH, *The Winner of Sorrow.*
D. KEITH MANO, *Take Five.*
MICHELINE AHARONIAN MARCOM,
  The Mirror in the Well.
BEN MARCUS,
  The Age of Wire and String.
WALLACE MARKFIELD,
  Teitlebaum's Window.
  To an Early Grave.
DAVID MARKSON, *Reader's Block.*
  Springer's Progress.
  Wittgenstein's Mistress.
CAROLE MASO, *AVA.*
LADISLAV MATEJKA AND KRYSTYNA
  POMORSKA, EDS.,
  Readings in Russian Poetics:
  Formalist and Structuralist Views.
HARRY MATHEWS,
  The Case of the Persevering Maltese:
  Collected Essays.
  Cigarettes.
  The Conversions.
  The Human Country: New and
  Collected Stories.
  The Journalist.
  My Life in CIA.
  Singular Pleasures.
  The Sinking of the Odradek
  Stadium.
  Tlooth.
  20 Lines a Day.
ROBERT L. MCLAUGHLIN, ED.,
  Innovations: An Anthology of
  Modern & Contemporary Fiction.
HERMAN MELVILLE, *The Confidence-Man.*
AMANDA MICHALOPOULOU, *I'd Like.*

FOR A FULL LIST OF PUBLICATIONS, VISIT:
www.dalkeyarchive.com

FOR A FULL LIST OF PUBLICATIONS, VISIT:
www.dalkeyarchive.com

Literature and Cinematography.
Theory of Prose.
Third Factory.
Zoo, or Letters Not about Love.
CLAUDE SIMON, The Invitation.
PIERRE SINIAC, The Collaborators.
JOSEF ŠKVORECKÝ, The Engineer of
    Human Souls.
GILBERT SORRENTINO,
    Aberration of Starlight.
    Blue Pastoral.
    Crystal Vision.
    Imaginative Qualities of Actual Things.
    Mulligan Stew.
    Pack of Lies.
    Red the Fiend.
    The Sky Changes.
    Something Said.
    Splendide-Hôtel.
    Steelwork.
    Under the Shadow.
W. M. SPACKMAN,
    The Complete Fiction.
ANDRZEJ STASIUK, Fado.
GERTRUDE STEIN,
    Lucy Church Amiably.
    The Making of Americans.
    A Novel of Thank You.
LARS SVENDSEN, A Philosophy of Evil.
PIOTR SZEWC, Annihilation.
GONÇALO M. TAVARES, Jerusalem.
LUCIAN DAN TEODOROVICI,
    Our Circus Presents . . .
STEFAN THEMERSON, Hobson's Island.
    The Mystery of the Sardine.
    Tom Harris.
JEAN-PHILIPPE TOUSSAINT,
    The Bathroom.
    Camera.
    Monsieur.
    Running Away.
    Self-Portrait Abroad.
    Television.
DUMITRU TSEPENEAG,
    The Necessary Marriage.
    Pigeon Post.
    Vain Art of the Fugue.
ESTHER TUSQUETS, Stranded.
DUBRAVKA UGRESIC,
    Lend Me Your Character.
    Thank You for Not Reading.
MATI UNT, Brecht at Night
    Diary of a Blood Donor.
    Things in the Night.
ÁLVARO URIBE AND OLIVIA SEARS, EDS.,
    Best of Contemporary Mexican
        Fiction.
ELOY URROZ, The Obstacles.
LUISA VALENZUELA, He Who Searches.
MARJA-LIISA VARTIO,
    The Parson's Widow.
PAUL VERHAEGHEN, Omega Minor.
BORIS VIAN, Heartsnatcher.
ORNELA VORPSI, The Country Where No
    One Ever Dies.
AUSTRYN WAINHOUSE, Hedyphagetica.

PAUL WEST,
    Words for a Deaf Daughter & Gala.
CURTIS WHITE,
    America's Magic Mountain.
    The Idea of Home.
    Memories of My Father Watching TV.
    Monstrous Possibility: An Invitation
        to Literary Politics.
    Requiem.
DIANE WILLIAMS, Excitability:
    Selected Stories.
    Romancer Erector.
DOUGLAS WOOLF, Wall to Wall.
    Ya! & John-Juan.
JAY WRIGHT, Polynomials and Pollen.
    The Presentable Art of Reading
        Absence.
PHILIP WYLIE, Generation of Vipers.
MARGUERITE YOUNG,
    Angel in the Forest.
    Miss MacIntosh, My Darling.
REYOUNG, Unbabbling.
ZORAN ŽIVKOVIĆ, Hidden Camera.
LOUIS ZUKOFSKY, Collected Fiction.
SCOTT ZWIREN, God Head.